Race Against Time

BOOKS BY GILBERT MORRIS

TIME NAVIGATORS
(Early Teen Fiction, ages 11–14)

1. *Dangerous Voyage*
2. *Vanishing Clues*
3. *Race Against Time*

THE HOUSE OF WINSLOW SERIES

1. *The Honorable Imposter*
2. *The Captive Bride*
3. *The Indentured Heart*
4. *The Gentle Rebel*
5. *The Saintly Buccaneer*
6. *The Holy Warrior*
7. *The Reluctant Bridegroom*
8. *The Last Confederate*
9. *The Dixie Widow*
10. *The Wounded Yankee*
11. *The Union Belle*
12. *The Final Adversary*
13. *The Crossed Sabres*
14. *The Valiant Gunman*
15. *The Gallant Outlaw*
16. *The Jeweled Spur*
17. *The Yukon Queen*
18. *The Rough Rider*
19. *The Iron Lady*
20. *The Silver Star*

THE LIBERTY BELL

1. *Sound the Trumpet*
2. *Song in a Strange Land*
3. *Tread Upon the Lion*
4. *Arrow of the Almighty*

CHENEY DUVALL, M.D.
(with Lynn Morris)

1. *The Stars for a Light*
2. *Shadow of the Mountains*
3. *A City Not Forsaken*
4. *Toward the Sunrising*
5. *Secret Place of Thunder*
6. *In the Twilight, in the Evening*

THE SPIRIT OF APPALACHIA
(with Aaron McCarver)

1. *Over the Misty Mountains*
2. *Beyond the Quiet Hills*

9705

Race Against Time

Gilbert Morris

BETHANY HOUSE PUBLISHERS
MINNEAPOLIS, MINNESOTA 55438

Race Against Time
Copyright © 1997
Gilbert Morris

Cover illustration by Chris Ellison

Published by Bethany House Publishers
A Ministry of Bethany Fellowship, Inc.
11300 Hampshire Avenue South
Minneapolis, Minnesota 55438

Printed in the United States of America.

Library of Congress Cataloging-in-Publication Data

CIP Data applied for

ISBN 1–55661–397–0   CIP

To Conan

GILBERT MORRIS spent ten years as a pastor before becoming Professor of English at Ouachita Baptist University in Arkansas and earning a Ph.D. at the University of Arkansas. During the summers of 1984 and 1985, he did postgraduate work at the University of London. A prolific writer, he has had over 25 scholarly articles and 200 poems published in various periodicals, and over the past years has had more than 70 novels published. His family includes three grown children, and he and his wife live in Texas.

1

"Watch this, Danny!" The small boy with blond hair and large blue eyes stared across the Parcheesi board, excitement etched on his thin face. "If I roll a six, it'll bring my last guy home!"

Danny Fortune smiled with affection at his brother, Jimmy. When it was his turn again, he picked up the dice and held them for a moment: "You know, don't you, that if I roll a two, I'll win," Danny said, amused at how intense his younger brother grew over the games they often played in the evening.

Although Danny was smiling, a line of worry creased his forehead. Even though Jimmy was bursting with excitement, he was looking very weak. He was five years old and had cystic fibrosis. The continual treatments he had to take for it were expensive, but the family had managed somehow.

"Go on, Danny! Roll the dice!" Dixie Fortune was Danny's twin. They had the same auburn hair and blue eyes. She was rather tall for a fourteen-year-old girl, which made her feel very self-conscious. There had been a time when she'd decided that she looked like an ugly giraffe. She had gone around stooped over until finally Danny grabbed her by the neck and pulled her upright, exclaiming, "Stand up straight, Dixie! For crying out loud, you look like a walking question mark! Besides, there are lots of girls who would love to be as tall as you. Look at all the models in the magazines!"

Dixie had snapped back, "I don't want to be one of those skinny models! I want to be petite and small . . . like Courtney Johnson!"

At least now Dixie had gotten over her hang-up about her height, and she sat cross-legged on the floor watching the other two finish the game. She had been too busy finishing her homework earlier to play with them.

"Come on, Jimmy. It's time to get to bed," Dixie announced firmly once Jimmy had won the game. She got to her feet, reached over, and helped her little brother up, saying, "I'll put the board away. You go brush your teeth and get your pajamas on."

"All right. I will." Jimmy rose and started out of the room. He looked over his shoulder at Danny and grinned. "You just wait till tomorrow. We'll play two games, and I'll beat you again. Both of 'em."

"Go brush your teeth," Danny warned him, "or I'll have to tickle you."

By the time Jimmy had come back, wearing a pair of Star Wars pajamas, his eyes were almost shut with sleepiness. "Good night, Dixie," he said, kissing her, and then he raised his arms to have Danny pick him up.

With Jimmy slung over his shoulder, Danny marched into the bedroom, held him for a moment, then counted, "One . . . two . . ." On the count of three, he tossed Jimmy onto the bed. Danny reached over and tousled the head of the boy who was already falling asleep, then quickly turned off the light and left the room.

He found his way into the kitchen, where Dixie was making hot chocolate. He got out the Ritz crackers and peanut butter and made little round sandwiches out of them, then the two walked back into the living room, plumped down on the overstuffed green couch, and sat there watching TV, waiting for Mom to get home.

They looked up suddenly as the sound of a door opening came from the hallway. "There's Mom," Dixie said. She got up and moved across the room quickly to meet her mother.

At the age of thirty-six, Ellen Fortune looked much younger than she actually was. She had blond hair and dark blue eyes, and she was taller than average. A smile leaped to her lips as she returned Dixie's hug and kissed her on the cheek.

"What have you been up to?" Mom asked.

"Oh, nothing. I just fixed tuna melts for supper, and the boys played Parcheesi. I'll heat up a sandwich for you."

"Hi, Mom." Danny came over and gave his mother a hug. She grunted, and he squeezed her even harder.

"Stop that! You're going to break my ribs!" she

joked. She moved into the kitchen, sat down, and listened as Danny and Dixie kept up a running conversation. When the meal was set before her, she said a quick prayer and, as usual, closed it with, "And bring James back, Lord."

Every night for over a week now, they had prayed for their father to come home. He was an associate history professor who had disappeared abruptly, leaving the family with no hint as to his whereabouts. While their mother prayed, however, Danny's and Dixie's eyes met as if they shared a secret. Danny nodded slightly but said nothing.

The three lingered around the table for a while longer, the twins sipping hot chocolate, and Ellen drinking decaf coffee. Finally she said, "Well, I'm going to shower and go to bed a little bit early. I'll see you two in the morning."

"Okay, Mom. Sleep well." Danny and Dixie looked at each other excitedly—here was their chance! They had told their eccentric inventor great-uncles that they'd visit that evening for a return trip back in time.

The two had actually gone back in time twice before. It had all come about when Danny had gone to see their great-uncles, Zacharias and Mordecai Fortune, to ask for help after their father had disappeared. To his shock, he discovered that Zacharias had invented a time machine, and that Mordecai, a famous historian, proposed sending them back in time to gather information. Danny had refused—until the uncles had promised to pay him and Dixie ten thousand dollars. But the big news came later, after the twins returned from their first eye-opening adventure. It was then that Mordecai and Zacharias confessed that James Fortune, who had been working for them, had traveled back in time—and gotten hopelessly lost.

As the twins began making their plans to slip away that night to their uncles' laboratory, Dixie suddenly doubled over, clutching her stomach.

"Oh, Danny, I don't feel well at all. I think I'm gonna throw up. Help me to the bathroom."

Danny scrambled to Dixie's side and walked with her as she tried to keep everything in. "Just hold on, Dix, we're almost there."

Ten minutes later, Dixie was sprawled out on her bed, a wet washcloth draped across her forehead. She was feeling a little better, but definitely not well enough for time travel.

"We haven't had the best of luck trying to find Dad," Danny complained as he sat on the bed with Dixie, keeping her company.

"No, but we know he's there somewhere. Sometime around the American Revolution." The Revolutionary War had been their father's favorite period of history, and they were almost positive he was in the Colonies somewhere during that time. But there was no telling in what year or in what part of the Colonies he had chosen to go.

On their first trip back in time, they had traveled on the *Mayflower* because Zacharias and Mordecai thought that James Fortune, who loved that period also, might be there. On their second trip, they had traveled to the time of the French and Indian Wars. They had met George Washington and some other famous figures but had found no trace of their father there, either.

Dixie shook her head. "Danny, I'm so sorry. What are we gonna do about the trip? We were supposed leave again tonight. I guess we'll have to call Mordecai and Zacharias and postpone things till I'm feeling better."

"Don't worry about it, Dix. You get your sleep, and we'll figure it out tomorrow. Maybe you'll be fine by the time school's out."

"Let's hope so," Dixie replied, her eyelids growing heavy with exhaustion. "The sooner we find Dad and bring him home, the better . . . for all of us."

Danny sighed, then got up and headed for the door. When he reached it, he turned around and said, "I wish our uncles had more sense. We wouldn't be in this mess if it weren't for them."

"Well, they're not stupid. After all, they invented a time machine."

Danny shrugged. "They may not be stupid, but they're definitely crazy."

"They may be, Danny, but they're the only chance we have. We'll have to make one more trip, at least, on the Chrono-Shuttle." She shook her head, thinking about the strange machine her uncles had invented that took them into the past. "It scares me to death every time I think of it, but God will take care of us."

Danny looked at her and said, "Well, before we do anything, you have to get over being sick. We can't go back to 1776 with the flu. You might infect the whole Continental Army!"

2

The halls of Calvin Coolidge Middle School were noisy and filled with students rushing to get to their first-period class. Danny had scrambled through his locker trying to find his notebook, which was buried under his gym equipment he had meant to take home the previous day. The socks gave off a sour smell, and Tony Paterno, whose locker was next to Danny's, held his nose and said, "Phew! What do you have in there? A litter of skunks?"

"Mind your own business, Tony!" Danny snapped. He plowed through the mess vowing, as he always did, to keep his locker cleaned out in the future, and he finally came up with his notebook. Slamming the door, he locked it, then made his way through the crowd headed for the stairs.

Danny's mind was far away from his schoolwork and filled with thoughts of Courtney Johnson. She was beautiful, popular, and, unfortunately, fifteen. He had followed her around for two years and spent a great amount of time mourning over the fact that she was a year older than he was.

Courtney had blond hair and blue eyes and came

from a very wealthy family. She already had a brand new red Mustang that was the envy of the entire student body. She couldn't drive it alone, since she only had her learner's permit. But she usually managed to find a sixteen-year-old with a license, whom she conveniently befriended.

As Danny reached the top of the stairs and turned toward his classroom, he was unaware of anything else going on around him. Courtney was in his next class, and he wanted to think of something to say that would impress her.

He reached Mrs. Simpkins' room at the same time as Tom Benton, the star quarterback of the football team. Benton slipped in beside him and gave him a hard shot with his hip. Danny was thrown sideways, and he dropped the armload of books he had been holding.

"Hey! Watch what you're doin', Benton!"

Tom Benton was tall and strong, and a sly grin spread across his face. "You should start watching me more during football practice. Then you'd learn how to fend off those blocks, Fortune."

Tom found his desk inside the classroom, and while Danny was picking up his books, a voice he recognized said, "Danny, what are you doing?"

Looking up quickly, Danny saw Courtney Johnson smiling down at him. She tilted her head to one side and looked so pretty that Danny could not speak for a moment. She was wearing a short, trendy dress. Courtney always looked like a model. Now as Danny scrambled to his feet and swallowed, he muttered, "Just dropped my books is all."

"Well, come on. We're going to be late."

"Uh . . . Courtney?"

"What is it, Danny?"

"How about going to a movie with me tonight?" Danny grimaced, hating how dumb he sounded. It was all he could think of to say before the late bell rang.

Courtney hesitated for a moment, then shrugged her shoulders. "Sorry, Danny. Tom Benton's already asked me to go."

Danny swallowed hard. "Well," he muttered, "maybe some other time."

Entering the room, he shot a nervous glance at Mrs. Simpkins as he made his way to the desk. She was thin, almost fifty, and hated tardiness. But most importantly, she was *always* right.

Slumping down in his seat, he opened his history book and scanned the lines of the chapter he was supposed to have read the night before. A guilty feeling came over him, and he thought, *I should have stayed up a little later and done my reading.*

Danny frantically scanned the pages of his history book as Mrs. Simpkins went through the attendance and other general announcements. Finally she began teaching the class, and Danny kept his ears half open trying to stay ahead of her.

Danny sat quietly until he heard Mrs. Simpkins talking about the crafts during the Colonial Period.

She spoke of silversmiths and goldsmiths, and then he heard her say, "The poor people had almost no silver or gold in those days, of course. As a matter of fact, they had almost nothing."

Danny suddenly remembered an incident that had happened on his last trip back in time. He and Dixie had stayed with a poor family for a while, and, hoping he would improve his grade, Danny raised his hand.

"What is it, Danny?" Mrs. Simpkins asked sharply, not at all liking the interruption.

"Well," Danny said quickly, "it's true that poor people didn't have silver and gold, but there were whitesmiths in those days."

"Whitesmiths?" Mrs. Simpkins' eyes widened, and she stared at him with disgust. "There's no such thing as a whitesmith! There're only goldsmiths and silversmiths!"

"Well, most people don't know about it, but tin was in short supply in those days, Mrs. Simpkins. A whitesmith was someone who worked with tin like a goldsmith works with gold and a silversmith with silver."

"I've never heard of such a thing!"

The class now turned to look at Danny. If Dixie had not had to stay home from school, she might have poked him in the back and hissed for him to be quiet. He was quickly getting himself into hot water.

Danny continued on with a step-by-step process of whitesmithing and finally ended his story, saying, "The stuff the whitesmiths made out of tin could get a disease."

Snickers erupted over the classroom, and Tom Benton said loudly, "You mean a tin cup could get the flu?" The laughter got even louder around the room, and Tom winked at Courtney. "I guess you'd have to take it to a tin doctor, wouldn't you?"

"That'll be enough out of you, Tom," Mrs. Simpkins said primly.

Danny looked over at Courtney and saw that she was laughing at him, too. How embarrassing! Infuriated, he said, "It's true! It got what they called 'tin plague.' The tin would disintegrate, so they had to put it in a blend of water and acid for six to eight hours."

"That's enough, Danny! I don't know how you come up with all that garbage," Mrs. Simpkins scolded. "It's time for the quiz. We'll see just how much you know about Colonial history, Mr. Fortune."

Danny was surprised at how well he did on the quiz even though he hadn't read the chapter. One good thing about his uncles' crazy invention was that going back in time sure helped with this history class—but he realized he also needed to do the reading. Obviously he wasn't going to have the chance to visit *every* period in history.

Unfortunately for the rest of the morning, every time he met any student that had been in his history class they would tease him about the tin disease. He was so sick of it by the time lunch hour came that he went to the cafeteria, got his food, and sat down at an empty table, hoping no one would sit by him.

Danny saw Tom Benton and Courtney sitting together. Benton caught his eye and raised his voice above the noise in the cafeteria. "Hey, I got a tin plate that's gettin' sick here! You better rush it to the tin doctor, Fortune!"

Danny's face burned as he saw Courtney laugh aloud. She made a half-hearted effort to stop the big quarterback, but Benton had a rough sense of humor, and all day, every time the two met, he pulled out the same old joke about the tin being sick.

Finally, after the last class, Danny gathered his books and smelly gym clothes into a bag and slammed his locker shut. As he left he saw Courtney heading out of the building. He was too humiliated to speak to her, but she turned and saw him, then said with a smile, "Hello, Danny."

"Hi, Courtney."

Courtney was usually surrounded by people, but this time they were both late getting out, and most everyone else was gone. "I guess you gave Mrs. Simpkins something to think about with the whitesmiths and sick tin and all."

"I'm getting really tired of hearing about that."

Courtney laughed. "You ought to know better by now, Danny. You've had these run-ins with her before. I remember when you had that big argument with her about the *Mayflower*."

"Well, she was wrong!" Danny snapped.

"You don't know that!"

"I do so!"

"How could you? You weren't there."

"Yes I was!"

Courtney stopped in her tracks, then turned to stare at him. "What are you talking about?"

"I mean, I was on the *Mayflower*."

Courtney's blue eyes widened. "Danny, don't be silly! That happened back in 1600 and something."

"Look, Courtney. I haven't told anybody about this," Danny blurted out, "but I can go back in time. My great-uncles have invented a time machine, and Dixie and I have already gone back twice."

Knowing that he was getting himself into trouble, Danny couldn't help but explain the whole story. He was so angry at being teased and so desperate to win Courtney's approval that he didn't care about the consequences. He told her about how his uncles had invented the Chrono-Shuttle and the details about how he and Dixie had gone back in time.

Courtney stood there listening, an odd look creeping onto her face. She had never spent much time talking to Danny because he was younger and not very popular. Now she didn't know what to think of him. She was amazed that he would say something so ridiculous.

"Do you really believe that, Danny?"

"Of course I believe it!" Danny snapped indignantly. "It's true!"

"It can't be!"

"I guess you'd have to see it for yourself," Danny maintained stubbornly. "As a matter of fact, I'm soon going to make another trip back in time to the Revolutionary War—Dixie and I."

"Well," Courtney said mockingly as she pushed a lock of blond hair behind her ear, "let me know when you get ready to go. I'd like to go with you."

"You think I'm crazy, don't you?"

"You're probably coming down with whatever your sister is sick with." Courtney laughed, then turned and said, "Don't forget. When you go back to visit the Revolution, take me with you."

Danny felt stupid. *Why did I have to tell her all that stuff? She must think I've really lost it.* He left the school and trudged toward home, thinking, *How dumb can I be? Not only will she never have anything to do with me, but she thinks I'm crazy, too.*

3

When Danny got home that afternoon, he found Dixie worse instead of better.

"I'll have to take her to the doctor tomorrow," his mother said. She had stayed home with Dixie all day, and there was a worried look on her face. "There's some kind of bad flu going around, and I'm afraid she's got it. You better stay out of her room, Danny. I don't want you to catch it, too."

Danny shook his head. "But I should help you take care of her."

"I don't need you sick, too," his mother said firmly. "Now, you just go on and finish your schoolwork and help with the chores. I'll be the nurse."

Danny reluctantly agreed, and the next day he again went to school without Dixie. He wondered if Courtney had said anything to anyone about the Chrono-Shuttle, and for the hundredth time he wished he had just kept his mouth shut.

He kept quiet in Mrs. Simpkins' history class that day and was surprised when Courtney fell into step beside him as they walked down the hall. "When are you going to make that trip back in time?" There was a teasing light in her eyes, and she added, "I hope I get to meet George Washington. I've always admired our first president."

"I'm really getting sick of you making fun of me, Courtney."

"Oh, Danny, relax. It's not every day I meet someone who travels through time."

That day after school, Courtney was working on her fashion column for the school newspaper. Danny had stayed for basketball practice, and he found her sitting on a bench on the front lawn of the school. Maybe if he tried talking to her one more time, her opinion of him would improve. He went and sat down beside her.

Courtney leaned back and studied him thoughtfully. "I didn't tell anybody about what you told me, Danny," she said finally. "They'd think you were crazy."

"Does that mean you think I'm crazy?" Danny had asked this before, but he had to know what she really thought.

"What am I supposed to think, Danny?"

"I'm not, you know. It's all the truth. Look, Courtney, if I showed you the Chrono-Shuttle, would you promise never to tell anybody about it?"

"So you're not giving up this silly idea?" Courtney asked.

"No way. Hey, why don't we go out to my uncles' house, and you can see the Chrono-Shuttle for yourself."

Courtney stared at him. He seemed so intent and honest, and finally she nodded. "All right. Let's go."

Danny instantly regretted inviting her. "Well . . . not right now," he stammered.

"Why not? I have my car here," Courtney said, her eyes daring him.

"But you don't have a license."

"Oh, I've driven by myself before. It's no big deal. Nobody's going to pay any attention to us."

"Yes they will! A red Mustang like that? If we get picked up, you'd probably get put in jail." Danny was beginning to panic.

"Hardly! My father would take care of it."

"I don't think we ought to do it."

"Are you going to chicken out? I thought you were so anxious to prove your story to me." Courtney got up and said, "Look, Danny. I'm tired of this. It's time for you to face up to reality."

Her attitude angered Danny. Pushing himself up off the bench, he stood in front of her and said, "All right, then! Let's go!"

Courtney stared at him. "You're really going through with this?"

"Of course I am! I've done it before . . . remember?"

Courtney was ready for the challenge, and she retorted, "Okay, let's go."

He walked with Courtney to her car and got into the passenger side of the red Mustang as Courtney got behind the wheel. She started the engine, then turned to him. "Which way?"

Danny could not ignore the warning bells his conscious was sending him for riding in a car with someone who didn't have her license, but he couldn't believe his luck that Courtney, the girl of his dreams, was offering him a ride. He started to give Courtney directions as she reached down and put the car into gear.

She pulled out of the parking lot, and they went roaring off, the wind blowing through their hair. "How do you like my car?" she asked with a flirty smile.

"Fine, but aren't you going a little fast?"

"Oh, this is nothing," Courtney said. "Wait until we get out of town. Then I'll really let her fly."

Danny's uncles lived outside of a very small town called Mayville. A bus route went right through it, which was the way that Danny and Dixie had always made the journey. They had to take a taxi to the house from town, though. This time, however, the trip was very quick because Courtney drove like a maniac the entire way.

"Aren't you worried your parents might find out about this?" Danny asked, his knuckles white from gripping the seat.

"Oh, they're gone on vacation. There's nobody in the house now except Mrs. Simms, our housekeeper, and she doesn't pay much attention to what I do."

"Where did they go?"

"They're on a cruise in the Caribbean. They'll be gone for another week. It's really been nice having the place to myself, Danny. I feel like an adult. I've been going where I please, and nobody's there to tell me what time to come home."

Danny looked ahead and motioned to a small road in the distance. "Turn off down on that dirt road."

"It'll ruin my wash job," Courtney whined.

"I'll wash it for you, Courtney," Danny promised.

They proceeded down the dirt road, and finally Danny pointed to his uncles' big home. "That's it over there."

"That old house?" Courtney pulled up in front and stared at it. "It looks like something from a horror movie." The old house itself was three stories tall, with spiraling turrets and huge windows. "Is it haunted?" Courtney asked.

"Of course not!" Danny got out impatiently, and Courtney followed. They walked up the steps to the high porch, and Danny rang the bell. As they waited he felt nervous, wishing he'd had better sense than to bring Courtney out to see his uncles. He wondered how they would react to him inviting a stranger over, or if they would even let Courtney see the Chrono-Shuttle. What if they wouldn't allow him the chance to prove his story to her?

The door swung open suddenly, and a gigantic man was framed in the entrance. "Hello, Toombs," Danny said quickly. "Are my uncles here?"

The giant lifted a hand that had banana-sized

fingers. He looked at them through slitted eyes and rumbled, "Yes." Stepping back, he escorted the two in. Glancing over, Danny saw that Courtney was subdued by the awesome size of the butler.

At that moment, a short man with a thin white beard and deep-set black eyes peeked out of another room. "Well, it's you, Danny." He came forward, then halted abruptly. "And who is this? I thought you were bringing your sister."

"No," Danny gulped nervously. "This is Courtney Johnson. Dixie's not feeling well." Then to Courtney he said, "This is my great-uncle, Zacharias Fortune."

Zacharias studied the young woman, then turned his sharp eyes on Danny. "You're not supposed to bring anybody else here."

"Well, I know," Danny stammered, "but I thought it might be all right. Courtney's very interested in science . . . aren't you, Courtney?"

"Uh . . . oh . . . yes, I am." Courtney was staring with wide-open eyes.

"Come along. You can meet my brother." Zacharias led them away from the front door.

They entered a room down the hall, and a head popped up from behind a mountain of books, papers, and magazines that littered a desk. "What's this?"

"This is my brother, Mordecai," Zacharias said to Courtney. Then to Mordecai, "Danny's here, and he's brought a visitor. A Miss Johnson."

"No visitors here!" Mordecai said. He was wearing an old suit that had once been blue but was so worn and faded it resembled a sack.

"No time for visitors. Sorry, come back later."

"But Uncle Mordecai," Danny pleaded, "can't I at least show Courtney the laboratory?"

An argument started, with Mordecai insisting that no visitors were needed while Zacharias was feeling more hospitable.

"After all, Mordecai," he said, "the young people have come a long way."

"Well, all right, but I have no time to waste." He stood up and cocked his head to one side. "Does she know about . . . you know what?"

"Yes, she knows about the Chrono-Shuttle. She's not quite sure about it, so I wanted her to see it."

"Come along," Zacharias said quickly. He turned, and his brother fell into step alongside him. They led Danny and Courtney through a long hallway, then down a long flight of steps to a huge room filled with dozens of weird-looking machines. In the center of the room, a large, glass-domed contraption was making strange whirling sounds.

"That's it, Courtney," Danny whispered, thrilled that he could share this important invention with her. "That's the Chrono-Shuttle."

Courtney was frightened by the strange people in the house, and there was something even more frightening about the laboratory. She whispered, "Danny, I don't like this."

"It's all right, Courtney. My uncles are a little bit

strange, but they're very smart. Come on and look at the Chrono-Shuttle."

As the two moved forward, Courtney saw that inside the clear glass machine, two chairs were positioned in front of some sort of a monitor. Wires laced through the glass tubing that wrapped around the back of its dome, and the whole machine was surrounded by an eerie green light.

Mordecai stepped up. He seemed to have suddenly remembered his manners. "We've been waiting for you, but obviously we expected your sister to come with you. Are you ready for another trip?"

"Well, not right now," Danny said. "I really should wait until Dixie's better."

"We have another idea of where your father could be," Zacharias added.

Courtney turned to stare at Danny. "What does he mean?" she demanded.

"Well, you see, my father was working for my uncles here, and they sent him back in time, but they can't get him home again. He's lost. That's why Dixie and I go back," he said earnestly. "We're trying to find him."

"But if he can't get back, how could you get back?" Courtney was somewhat shocked to find herself talking as if time travel were even possible. There was something utterly convincing about the laboratory and the two strange scientists who stood before her. "Tell me more about your father."

Mordecai took over, explaining, "Well, Mr. James

Fortune is our nephew and quite a historian in his own right. We paid him to help us with research, and when it came time to test out our Chrono-Shuttle, he volunteered to go."

"But we hadn't quite put the finishing touches on our invention," Mordecai's twin cut in. "We had not had much success with a method of getting people back. Easy enough to send people," he shrugged, "but getting them back proved to be difficult."

"But they invented a Recall Unit," Danny took over. "When anyone goes into time, they take a Recall Unit with them. When they want to come home, all they have to do is press the button and they're back."

Courtney was fascinated. "Does it really work?" she asked excitedly.

"Of course it works," Zacharias snapped. He placed a hand on the Chrono-Shuttle and gave it a pat. "I don't invent things that don't work—not usually, that is," he added sheepishly, remembering that he was responsible for James being lost.

"But your father didn't get back."

"He couldn't because he didn't have a good Recall Unit. All we have to do now is find him, then he can come home with us."

Danny continued to explain the situation to Courtney, and the two old men stood there listening impatiently.

"This is so exciting. I didn't believe a word of it before," Courtney gasped. "When are you going to go back?"

"Well, I don't know," Danny said. "Dixie's sick right now, and we've always gone together."

"I'd think you'd have courage enough to go back on your own! After all, he is your father!" Zacharias was trying to make Danny feel guilty.

"And after all, you're the two who got him lost in time," Danny shot back. "Hopefully Dixie will be well in a few days."

"That's a long time for your father to have to wait," Mordecai said. "Why don't you just go now?"

"I can't do it now."

"Why not?" Mordecai asked.

"Wouldn't you be gone for weeks?" Courtney asked in confusion.

"Actually, I wouldn't be gone long at all," Danny told her. "Something's different about time when you go to the past. For instance, we went to Plymouth and sailed on the *Mayflower*. That took months, but when we came back, only a few hours had passed."

"I see," Courtney said excitedly. "So you could spend a year there and only be gone five minutes of our time?"

"That's it exactly!" Mordecai said quickly. "It's all a part of my plan. What I want to do is to prove that history, as we learn it now, is sometimes wrong. So we send someone back, get the actual facts, and then bring them back to give us the correct information."

"Why don't *you* go, Mr. Fortune?" Courtney challenged.

The idea seemed to insult Mordecai. "Why, I'm

much too valuable a scholar to risk my life, and I'm too old anyway. But Danny here, he's young, and he's got a big investment. His own father's out there. Really, Danny, I think you ought to go. It's your duty."

"Yes, exactly!" Zacharias agreed. "And we're all set up and ready for you to go right now."

"You don't know where or when to send me," Danny said. "You're just making guesses."

"Your father was always anxious to find out more about Valley Forge," Mordecai said. "I'm certain that's where he is."

"So you're willing to risk my life because you're certain?" Danny questioned, a hint of sarcasm in his voice. "I can't go alone. There needs to be two of us. We found that out before."

"You don't have to go alone," Courtney suddenly spoke up.

Danny looked at her, startled. "What are you talking about?"

"I'll go with you."

"No way!" Danny held firm. "You can't do that!"

"Yes, I can," Courtney said. She was, indeed, very determined, and for half an hour she argued with Danny about it. "I really want to see if this thing actually works."

"Why, I think it would be excellent for this dear girl to accompany you," Zacharias said quickly. "Don't you think so, Mordecai?"

"Certainly! Now, that ends this discussion."

"All right," Danny finally agreed. "If you're sure

you want to do it, Courtney. But it could be dangerous, and I know it'll be rough and dirty. I don't think
you have any idea what you're getting into."

"I can do anything you can do, Danny Fortune!"
Courtney exclaimed.

"Well, if you insist," Danny conceded. His heart
began to race with excitement at the thought of going
back in time with Courtney. He turned to his uncles
and added, "Be sure to let Dixie know right away after
we've gone."

"Oh, certainly. We'll take care of that," Mordecai
Fortune beamed. "Now all you need to do is change
your clothes into more appropriate attire."

"Well, I guess we're ready, then," Danny said after
he had changed.

Courtney sighed when she came out of the bathroom wearing a simple gray dress and bonnet. "Could
these clothes be any uglier?" she complained, picking
at a fold in her skirt. "And the shoes—I can't figure out
how I'm supposed to walk in these clumsy things."
Courtney glared at Danny, who suddenly felt less sure
about taking her with him. "If I break my ankle, it'll
be all your fault!"

"I . . . I think you look great, Courtney," he gulped.
*And besides, I really need your help if I'm going to find
Dad before it's too late*, he added to himself.

Mordecai huffed. "I hate to interrupt you two, but

Zacharias and I have other important business to take care of this afternoon, so if we could begin. . . ." He steered them toward the Chrono-Shuttle. "And just in case, here is a pouch of gold coins. They should do the trick—although I don't want you getting the idea that you can spend them on just *anything*."

Mordecai and Zachariah then brought out the Recall Unit, which was tied to a leather cord, and slipped it over Danny's head.

Danny examined it, then held it up for Courtney. "When I press this button, we have to be standing together. Otherwise, you'll be marooned in time."

A shiver went through Courtney at that word, but she was determined not to let her fright be seen. Mordecai opened the door, and the two got into the Chrono-Shuttle. It was like sitting in the backseat of a big car. In front of them were simple controls and gauges, but Zacharias gave them no chance to examine them further. He reached up and pulled down a red lever.

Courtney cried out slightly. Danny reached over and took her hand, saying, "It's all right. Don't be afraid."

But Courtney was afraid. The room was immediately filled with a strange light, and the vibrations grew very powerful. An eerie green glow filled the Chrono-Shuttle, and Courtney suddenly turned and grabbed at Danny. He put his arm around her.

As Courtney glanced outside, it seemed as if the uncles were vanishing, and even the lab itself seemed to be dissolving! The shrill humming increased until it hurt her ears, and suddenly she felt as if she were falling through space. *Maybe this is all a trick*, she thought wildly and tried to get out. But by then it was too late.

4

The first thing Courtney felt as the green haze seemed to fade away was an intense, biting cold. She was aware that she was no longer sitting in a leather-covered seat but was lying full-length on what felt like a soft mattress. She was extremely cold. Her hands contracted, and her eyes flew open as the cold bit into them. Sitting straight upright, she saw that she was sitting on a blanket of snow at least six or seven inches deep. She looked around wildly, seeing the huge trees burdened with masses of snow that almost blotted out the blue sky above.

"Danny!" she cried out quickly, fear running through her, and she was relieved at a voice behind her calling her name. Whirling around, she saw Danny getting to his feet and brushing the snow from his clothes.

"I didn't think it'd be this cold," he shivered. "I should have remembered that at Valley Forge the soldiers nearly froze to death. Are you all right, Courtney?"

"I . . . I guess so." Getting to her feet, Courtney looked down at the roughly made shoes and saw that the snow sank in over the tops. "My shoes are full of snow."

"Mine, too. Come on. Let's see if we can get out of here and find a road. Maybe the snow won't be so deep."

The two floundered on through the snow, shaken by the bitter wind.

"You'd think my uncles would have had enough sense to give us heavy coats," he muttered. Both Danny and Courtney were wearing lightweight coats made of wool, but the wind cut right through them.

Before they had traveled more than fifteen minutes, Courtney's teeth were chattering, and her face was so stiff that she could hardly move her lips. "I . . . I've got to get out of this, Danny. I'll freeze to death."

Danny agreed, for the fierce wind seemed to go right through to his skin. "Come on, let's keep moving. We can't stay in these woods. We'll find a road sooner or later."

"How did your uncles know where to put us down when they sent us here?" Courtney pulled the light jacket closer over her chest.

"They use latitude and longitude. The crucial thing is we don't want to materialize in the middle of a brick wall or something like that. So far we've been lucky, but this time—hey, look! There's a road!"

The two hurried out of the forest, and the sky overhead was blue-gray with a few white, fluffy clouds high above. The road had been heavily traveled; brown mud marred the whiteness of the snow.

"There have been wagons along here, and horses," Danny said eagerly. "Come on. It's got to go somewhere."

After trudging along the road for half an hour, Courtney looked up and squealed, "Look! There's a town!"

"Sure is," Danny said. "How are your feet?"

"I can't even feel them."

"I can't, either. My legs feel like they belong to somebody else. It's not far, though."

The two made their way down the road, stumbling in the deep ruts on their numb feet, and as they came closer, Danny said, "It's just a small village, but there's got to be someplace we can warm up and get something to eat."

The town had only one street with several shops and businesses on each side. Farther down they saw houses crowded close together. It appeared to be a town hacked out of the wilderness, with large trees bordering it except for the fields on the far side where the land had been cleared.

"Look, Danny. That seems like a place that might have food."

Danny looked up and saw the sign swinging on an iron rod. It had no words, but there was a picture of a blue horse on it. "That must be the Blue Horse Tavern."

"We're going to a *saloon*?"

"If we get anything to eat and a place to stay, it'll be at a saloon," Danny guessed.

The two took in the sights on the street and noted a few people scattered about. They reached the Blue Horse Tavern and gratefully made their way inside the warm main room. Courtney and Danny took in their surroundings as they let the feeling come back to their feet and hands. It was a large, single room with a long counter along one side. On the other wall a huge fireplace threw out warmth as the logs crackled and sparks flew up the chimney. There were half a dozen tables and several mismatched chairs scattered around, and the ceiling was so low a tall man would have hit his head on the beams that were turned black with age.

"Well, now. What can I do for you young'uns?"

Danny and Courtney turned quickly to see a large, burly man who had come out of the door on the back wall. He was wearing a rather dirty white apron, and his face was rosy. He had short, cropped iron gray hair and a pair of sharp, black eyes.

"We'd like a place to stay tonight . . . and something to eat."

"Well, I think that can be arranged. You got any money?" the innkeeper added suspiciously.

"Oh yes!" Danny pulled out a coin and handed it to him.

The man took it, bit it, then said, "Good hard money. My name's Ebenezer Taylor." He handed the coin back to Danny and peered at the two. "One room? I got a nice room upstairs. Good, sound bed. Fresh corn shucks."

"We'll need two rooms," Danny said.

Courtney shot a startled glance at Danny, who appeared to be used to such things.

"Oh yes. You can sleep in the other vacant room. Probably won't be too crowded tonight."

"Could we get something to eat right away?" Courtney said, finding she was very hungry.

"Sure thing. Me wife's cooked a fresh haunch of venison. If you care to clean up, there's a washstand upstairs."

The two went upstairs and looked inside the rooms, each of which contained one bed. Courtney punched it, and the mattress made a crackling sound. "What's this mattress made out of?" she asked curiously.

"Stuffed with corn shucks. Underneath you won't find springs." Danny grinned.

Courtney leaned over and looked at the underside, finding that the springs consisted of ropes tied tightly together, forming a sort of knit. "Well, I've never slept on anything like this before!"

They moved to the washstand and took turns washing, then dried on a rather dirty towel.

When they went back downstairs, a large, rather heavyset woman came out. She was wearing a gray dress that touched the floor with a white apron over it and a bonnet. Her face was as round and rosy as her husband's. "Sit you down," she insisted and put before them a platter of roasted meat and a bowl.

"What's in the bowl?" Courtney whispered.

"Probably corn," Danny answered. "You can almost count on having corn in Colonial times."

The two started eating and found that the meat, though overcooked, was delicious. The corn was good, too, and the fresh-baked bread was the best of all.

The innkeeper came and put down two pewter tankards and said, "Fresh cider. Best in the county."

Danny tasted it and nodded with a smile. "It is good." They sat there drinking the cider and soaking up the warmth in the cozy room. Finally Danny said, "It's getting dark outside. We've got to figure out how to find Washington's camp at Valley Forge."

His question was cut off at the sound of horses approaching. Rising to his feet, Danny went to the window and peered out. "It's a coach—looks like it's loaded."

Soon the tap room was filled with travelers—five men and three women all bundled up in heavy clothing.

The innkeeper and his wife were busy serving them, and Danny made conversation with a rather tall, thin man wearing a black suit and a tall stovepipe hat. The man looked very carefully at Danny and said, "Your speech is strange. I don't recognize your accent."

"Oh, we come from farther north," Danny quickly recovered. The man's accent was strange, too, and Danny remembered the way people spoke during this time period. He looked over at Courtney, who seemed fascinated by all of this, then asked the man, "Have you heard anything about the war?"

The tall man, whose name was Smith, shook his head. "War? I'd not call it a war. A rabble in arms. That's what it is."

Several around the table nodded their agreement. A large, beefy man stuffed a huge piece of venison into his mouth and spoke around it. "The British will soon get rid of Washington and his ragtag little army. They nearly did it in New York."

Smith took a swallow of ale and nodded. "Can't last long. Washington lost most of his army. The general could finish it now, but there's no rush."

"Where is the army now? Washington's, I mean," Danny fished for information.

"Oh, somewhere close around here. Innkeeper, where's Washington and that rabble of his?"

"They's holed up in Valley Forge," Ebenezer said.

"It'll be over in spring. The British will bring their troops out, and that'll be all of it," Smith concluded.

One of the ladies, a small woman with a pinched face and who was rather poorly dressed, said mildly, "I'm not sure the British will win."

"Emily, be quiet! No one asked your opinion!" snapped a man beside her, obviously her husband.

Danny cast a glance at Courtney and resolved to say no more.

After the travelers had feasted, the driver of the coach instructed, "Better get to bed. We leave at dawn."

At the mention of sleep, Courtney swallowed a yawn and excused herself from the table. She was exhausted and could hardly wait to collapse into bed. She moved upstairs and entered the room, then turned around—startled as the three women who had arrived on the coach followed her in. The small woman smiled at her. "Well, it'll be a rather tight fit for four of us."

The other two women were quite large. One of them sniffed, "I'll be surprised if the bed doesn't break down!"

Courtney was furious. She had brought no clothes with her except what she wore, and the women all put on heavy nightgowns and at once got into bed. She looked at it and said, "I think I'll just roll up in a blanket on the floor. That way you'll have more room."

The two large women nodded their agreement, but the smaller one said, "It'll be hard for you sleeping on the floor, my dear."

Courtney ignored the comment and grabbed some blankets, wrapped up in them, and spent the night rolling around, trying to find a comfortable position. She couldn't find one, however, and when dawn came she was the first one out of the room.

She found Danny downstairs already. "How was your sleep, Courtney?"

She glared at him. "Horrible. I slept on the floor. My back feels like one big knot. How about you?"

"I slept on the floor, too. A little bit crowded in that

one bed. Not like taking a vacation at Disneyland, is it?"

Courtney knew he was getting back at her for her disbelief in his story about the Chrono-Shuttle. She ignored him and asked, "What do we do now?"

"We've got to get to Valley Forge. I've already had some breakfast. You eat, and I'll go out and buy us a horse."

"A horse! I can't ride a horse!"

"Well, maybe I can get a buggy."

While Danny was out, Courtney ate a large breakfast, which consisted of some sort of corn, fried bacon, and eggs. Not knowing when she would get a meal again, she ate heartily. Afterward the travelers came down, ate, and left in the coach.

Twenty minutes after the coach pulled out, Courtney looked up to see Danny walk through the door. "I got us a buggy," he said. "Now we have to find out how to get to Valley Forge. Innkeeper?" he shouted.

Ebenezer came from the back room and nodded.

"How much do we owe you?"

"Two and sixpence."

Danny had no idea what that was, but he took the change back from the innkeeper and asked, "Can you tell me how to get to Valley Forge?"

Ebenezer's sharp eyes narrowed. "Why would you be wantin' to go there?"

"Oh, we've heard a lot about George Washington,"

Danny explained quickly. "Just thought we might go by and meet him."

"I wouldn't advise it, but if you've got to go, I can tell you the way."

5

"Man, it's freezing!" Danny said, shivering and pulling his coat closer around him. They had stopped at a store in the small village and spent one of the gold coins on warm coats, heavy socks, and warm long underwear. Now as the horse trotted along, sending small clouds of light, fluffy snow behind him, Danny looked over and studied Courtney. She had said almost nothing on their journey, and there was a pinched, tight look around her mouth. "Are you warm enough?" Danny asked.

"I'm all right."

Courtney's answer was very short, and as the buggy made its way through the drifts, Danny suspected she missed being at home. She was usually very talkative, and he could tell something was wrong. Finally he broke the silence. "Are you afraid, Courtney?"

Glancing at him quickly, Courtney's mouth relaxed. She nodded briefly and answered, "I . . . I guess so. I've never done anything like this before."

"Well, most people haven't." Danny tried to appear relaxed, but seeing her fear he said, "I think it's always like this. Both times when Dixie and I came back into the past we were scared during the entire trip."

"Were you really?"

"Sure. Who wouldn't be?"

"It helps a little bit to know you're scared, too." She moved over a fraction closer to him on the seat and looked out over the landscape. "Do you know where we're going?"

"Just what the innkeeper said. We turned off the main road, and we ought to be coming to Valley Forge any time."

"What are we going to do when we get there?" Courtney asked nervously.

"We'll just have to wing it," Danny said, shrugging his shoulders. "You know, if it were different circumstances this might almost be fun. I hope we won't be here too long, though. It would be so great if we could walk into that camp and find my dad the first day!"

"Do you think that's possible?"

Danny slapped the horse's rump with the reins. Although he had never done it before, he was good at driving. "I doubt it," he admitted. "Most things don't work out the way you want them to."

"They usually do for me."

Danny shot Courtney a quick glance, thinking about how simple her life must be. Her parents probably gave her anything she asked for. Then his gaze softened, and he couldn't help but notice how pretty she looked in the morning light. He felt excited just sitting by her. This first leg of their trip had been a little crazy, but now that they were on their way to the camp and Danny had time to think about things, he realized again how much he liked Courtney. *What would she do if I held her hand right now?* But Danny quickly buried that thought . . . for now. He didn't want to do anything to ruin things between them.

They drove along for a while longer, then suddenly Danny spoke up. "Look, Courtney. There's some soldiers and some buildings down there."

Looking up, Courtney squinted her eyes against the bright sunlight that reflected off the snow. "It doesn't look like an army to me. They're not in uniform."

Courtney was right. As they drew closer, they both saw that the men were wearing nothing but rags. "Why, they look horrible!" Courtney exclaimed. "They can't be soldiers!"

"I think they are," Danny said soberly. "Remember what we read about in history class? This was a tough time for them. Most of the soldiers in Washington's army never got uniforms, or at least not until the very end of the Revolution. Look, some of them are coming out to meet us."

Four men put themselves in a line across the road, all of them holding their muskets. One, larger than the rest, stood out in front of the others. His clothes were made up of remnants of garments of all kinds and seemed to be stuffed with rags so that he bulged out. He had on a pair of gloves, but the fingers were cut out, and his exposed fingers were blue from the cold of the December wind. He had a heavy, round face and a pair of small, muddy brown eyes that peered suspiciously at them. Holding up his musket he shouted, "Halt or be shot!"

Instantly Danny pulled the horse to a stop and cleared his throat nervously. "Hello," he said, hoping no one heard his voice cracking from fear.

The soldier turned his head slightly and winked at the man next to him, a small man with a fur cap and a musket that seemed too big for him. "Well now, Silas. What have we got here?"

The man named Silas returned the wink. "I tell you, Jake," he said with a snicker, "it looks like we got supper."

The smaller man moved forward and put his hand on the shoulder of the horse. He grinned, showing broken, yellow teeth, and patted the horse, nodding with satisfaction. "He'll make a right smart breakfast for our company, won't he, Jake?"

"Reckon he will." The big man named Jake walked around and suddenly reached up and grabbed Danny by the arm. Before Danny could move, he found himself pulled from the buggy. "Hey, let go of me!"

Courtney sat there paralyzed with fear, and the two other soldiers came around, both of them tall men with wolfish-looking eyes. "Hey, missy. You're a pretty one, ain't you? Why don't you come off of there and come with us. We'll share our supper with you. We'll be good company for you." He winked at his companion, then suddenly reached out and pulled

Courtney from the buggy. The big man they called Jake moved to hold the harness of the horse, and he called out, "Maitland, you go take this horse and butcher him up. Don't tell everybody about it or there won't be none left for us."

"You can't do that!" Danny cried. He struggled to free himself from the big man's grasp, but the soldier's hand was like iron.

"Why don't you turn around and go on back where you came from, sonny?" the burly soldier snarled. He looked over to where Courtney was being held, each of the soldiers gripping her arms. "We'll take care of your lady friend here."

Courtney was struggling in vain as the two soldiers grinned down at her. "Let me go!" she panted.

"Don't play hard to get, girlie. We Virginia men know how to treat a lady right." The two were wearing fringed shirts, and their rifles looked different from the muskets. They were the famous long rifles that the Virginia troops had brought into the service with them. Danny knew that the Virginians gave Washington a great deal of trouble. Although they were from his own state, they were rebellious and almost impossible to command. In a fight they were fierce warriors, but Danny had read that Washington had almost given up any hope of getting them to work as a team.

The man called Maitland started to lead the horse off, and Courtney cried out, "Danny!"

A dirty, hard hand suddenly closed over Courtney's

mouth, and she was held so tightly that she could not move. "Come on," Silas said. "We'll show this little lady some hospitality."

With a mighty effort, Courtney turned her head to one side and began to scream. Instantly it was cut off, and Jake yelled, "Keep her quiet!"

Danny broke free from the burly man who was holding him and ran toward Courtney. *Maybe if I could just touch her and hit the recall button, we'd get out of this mess.* But he realized almost instantly that he couldn't take the chance of bringing the soldiers back with them.

As he reached the trio, a fist caught him on the temple and he went down. The world seemed to revolve in stars, and he felt his back hit the hard-packed snow. At the same time he heard a different voice say, "What's going on here, men?"

Courtney managed to turn and see a man wearing a uniform and a three-cornered hat. He had appeared, seemingly, from nowhere, and when he got closer she saw that his eyes were an intense violet. He was a small man, but there was an air of command about him, and his voice crackled with authority as he said, "Turn that girl loose!"

Instantly Courtney was released, and the two men backed away, saluting as they did.

"Well, sir," the big man called Jake began and tried to bluff his way through an explanation. "We caught these two. They must be spies. We was going to bring 'em to you so you could question 'em."

"That's a lie!" Danny said, his eyes flashing. He slowly got to his feet and added, "They were going to kill our horse for food, and who knows what would have happened to Courtney if you hadn't shown up."

The officer's eyes seemed to glow with fire. "You know better than to mistreat visitors. His Excellency has given firm orders about that."

"But, sir—"

"Shut your mouth, Wilkins! You and these other men get on down the road. See if you can act like soldiers for a change."

The four men quickly moved away, the smaller one named Silas throwing a venomous glance back at Danny and Courtney.

I'd hate for him to catch me alone, Danny thought. Then he turned to the officer and said, "Thank you very much, sir. We were in real trouble."

"Please accept my apology. Those men are good soldiers in a battle, but their manners are rough. I'm Colonel Hamilton."

Could it be Alexander Hamilton? Danny thought back to his history quiz. This was the man that would later play an important role in the formation of a new country. He would become a rival with Thomas Jefferson, and the two men would engage in a mighty struggle to see what kind of a country America would become.

"What are you doing here, young man? What's your name?"

"My name is Danny Fortune, and this is my friend Courtney Johnson."

"What are you doing out here away from home? Don't you know there's a war on?"

"Yes, sir. We know that, but I've come looking for my father."

"Your father?" Colonel Hamilton's eyes narrowed. "What would your father be doing out here?"

"Well, I'm not exactly sure, sir." He improvised quickly, saying, "We think he might be with the Continental Army. He left home some time ago, and my mother needs his help. We all do."

"What's his name?"

"James Fortune."

Hamilton frowned. "I don't know the name, but, of course, I don't know all the men." He hesitated for a moment. "Come along. I can't leave you here." He looked at the horse, and a slight smile touched his lips. "Bringing that horse into this camp is like taking a side of cooked Virginia ham into a prison."

"I . . . I didn't think of that, Colonel Hamilton."

"Well, come along. We'll go to our headquarters. It's right over there."

The headquarters, which was actually an old house that was used by the officers, was unimpressive. All around there were rows of hastily built huts, mostly made of logs and being little more than crude shelters. Hamilton led them to the front of the farmhouse, took the salute of the sentry on charge, and asked, "Owens, do you have a man named James Fortune in your unit?"

"No, sir. Nobody that I know of with that name."

"Ask around, will you? These young people are looking for him."

"Yes, sir."

Hamilton mounted the steps, opened the door, and allowed Danny and Courtney to go inside. It was a typical rough cabin, larger than most, and several officers were gathered in front around the fire.

"Gentlemen, we have visitors," Hamilton said. The men turned. "This young man is looking for his father—James Fortune. Do any of you have him in your company?"

A tall, portly man with a handkerchief wrapped around one hand turned. "What was the name again?"

"Fortune. James Fortune, Colonel."

Colonel Knox had a broad, round face and a pleasant expression. "Fortune . . . hmmm. No, I believe I'd remember a name like that."

"How about you, Colonel Greene? This is Nathan Greene," Hamilton added in introduction.

Greene was a tall, raw-boned man with a rugged face. He ran his fingers through his thinning hair and shook his head. "Don't know the name. Are you sure he's with the army here?"

"No, sir, I'm not. But he's been missing, and I'm pretty sure he joined up."

Knox grinned and said, "We haven't had too many volunteers lately, have we gentlemen?"

Greene shook his head. "No. We've lost more than we've gained."

"We'll have plenty of volunteers when the spring comes," Hamilton sounded hopeful.

"Pray God it may be so," Knox nodded.

"Is the general inside?"

"Yes, he is," Knox answered.

Stepping over to the door, Colonel Hamilton knocked, and a voice said, "Come in."

Hamilton opened the door and nodded to Danny and Courtney, and the two stepped inside. Danny stopped in front of a small desk, where a man sat writing. He recognized Washington instantly. It had been twenty-two years of Washington's time since he had met him, but there was always a chance he might remember Danny. He and Dixie had visited Washington's plantation and had stayed for a while with him and his wife, Martha. But Danny hoped that Washington would have forgotten him.

"Excuse me, sir, these two came in search of this young man's father. They think he may be a soldier in the ranks."

Washington put down the turkey quill pen and got to his feet. Courtney was speechless. She had read about George Washington, but to look at him in the flesh was too exciting for words. He was, she saw, a very tall man, wide at the hips, muscular shoulders, and his face looked exactly like some of the paintings she had seen of him. It was a stern face, but there was an air of kindness about Washington as he said,

"Welcome to Valley Forge. You say you are looking for your father?"

"Yes, sir. My name is Danny Fortune, and my father's name is James."

"And who is this young lady?"

"This is Courtney Johnson, General Washington. A neighbor of mine."

Washington turned his blue-gray eyes on Danny and studied him. "You know, I once knew a young man very much like you—and had the same name, if I'm not mistaken. But then, I must be wrong, for that young man was searching for his father, too. . . ." He shook his head and continued, "However, that was a long time ago, and I may not remember all the details correctly. No word about your father?"

"No, sir. Not yet." Danny's nerves died down when the general seemed to give up on putting the two together. "General, I'm sure my father is somewhere in this part of the country."

"How did he come to leave home without telling you where he was going? You have a mother, I suppose?"

"Yes, sir, and she's very worried about him. We all are. I have a younger brother and a sister. My brother's not well, and we need to find my father as soon as we can. We just assumed he would have joined your ranks, General. He always spoke so highly of you."

"Well, we can have the quartermaster check the rolls. If your father's enlisted in this service, I think we can find him easily enough. We've had a little trouble with the records, however." A wry look came to his eyes. "We had to leave headquarters in New York rather abruptly."

Colonel Hamilton suddenly broke in. "We never should have been there in the first place. That place was indefensible."

"Now, Colonel Hamilton, we've been over that. Would you see to our young friends here?"

"Yes, sir."

Washington moved forward and put his hand out. "I pray that you will find your father. If I can be of any help, don't hesitate to call." He turned to Courtney and bowed slightly.

Courtney was almost petrified, but she knew that she would never again have the chance to shake hands with George Washington. Impulsively she put her hand out. To her amazement, Washington bowed low and kissed her hand. "You should be very careful with a pretty, young lass like this, Mr. Fortune," Washington smiled. He released Courtney's hand and stepped back.

Danny and Courtney moved out of the room, and when they were outside, Hamilton was asking Colonel Knox, "Where's Lieutenant Masters?"

"I think he went down to the hospital. His brother's there, you know. Not doing well," Knox replied.

"Lieutenant Masters is our quartermaster," Hamilton told Danny and Courtney. "He'll have the list, but we'll have to find him first."

"Could we go to the hospital?" Danny asked, realizing it was possible that his father was there.

"I wouldn't want you going alone," Colonel Hamilton warned. "I need to visit a few of the men myself. Come along."

The three of them went outside, and Danny and Courtney were shocked by the conditions of the men they passed. They were all wearing little more than rags, some of them had shoes bound on with leather cords, and a few of them had toes exposed that had turned blue with the cold.

Colonel Hamilton stopped before a long, low building built of logs. He turned suddenly, saying, "Miss Johnson, you may not want to go in. It's not very pleasant inside."

"Oh, I'll be fine, Colonel," Courtney replied quickly, not wanting to be separated from Danny in this strange, rustic place.

Still Hamilton argued, "It doesn't smell too good, I'm afraid. We don't have any modern facilities here, no medicine to speak of, and the men are hungry. Perhaps it would be better if you didn't go in."

But Courtney insisted, and as Hamilton opened the door, she stepped through it. She was at once assaulted by the terrible odor of men closely packed in without any sanitary facilities. There were a few on cots, but most of the patients were on the floor on rags of what used to be blankets. She shrank back, and Danny stepped close beside her and took her arm. He squeezed it with encouragement, and she looked at him, her eyes wide with a mixture of fear and disgust.

A tall man with a white apron covered with dried blood stepped forward at once.

"Ahh, Colonel Hamilton. Come to visit the men. That's good."

"Yes, I do have a few moments, but I'm looking for Lieutenant Masters."

"He's down at the end talking to his brother."

"Doctor Simmons, this is Danny Fortune and Courtney Johnson. They're here looking for Danny's father."

"He's in the army?"

"That's why we have to find Lieutenant Masters."

"Well, go right along. The men will be glad to see you. They get lonely, you know." Simmons had a defeated look in his eye. "If I just had some medicine, plenty of blankets, and warm food, I could do more to help them." He cast a pitiful glance across the room.

Hamilton put his hand on the doctor's thin shoulder. "You're doing a fine job, Simmons. No man could do more."

"We need supplies so badly, Colonel. Is there any hope of getting some?"

Hamilton bit his lip and shook his head. "We can always hope," he said briefly, then turned to Danny and Courtney. "You two, perhaps, had better wait here."

Hamilton strolled off quickly, walking down the middle of the long building.

Dr. Simmons eyed his two young visitors. "Are you

from this part of the country?"

"Well, not too far away," Danny answered.

"I don't have an office for you to wait in. Would you like to talk to some of the men?"

Danny hesitated, then nodded.

"Well, there's one young soldier I think might be helped by a visit. His name is Nathaniel Bates. Come along."

"Is he very sick, doctor?"

"He was wounded in the last engagement at White Plains," Dr. Simmons said. "We got the musket ball out, but he hasn't recovered well. He's very young, and he misses his mother. Only seventeen."

Dr. Simmons led the way to a section of the hospital that was built off the back of the main building. It was only ten by fifteen, more or less, and only four patients were in there.

"Well, Nathaniel. Would you do with a little company?"

The young soldier was lying on a rough cot built of saplings with a piece of canvas stretched across it. He had fair hair and very large light blue eyes. "I guess so, Doc."

"You visit with Nathaniel while Colonel Hamilton is busy," the doctor said. He turned and walked away without another word.

Danny swallowed hard and stepped forward. "I'm sorry that you got hurt, Mr. Bates."

The young man smiled faintly. He had a pleasant face, but as he waved his hand, they saw it was as thin as a skeleton. "Just Nathaniel," he whispered. He looked at the two and said, "Who are you? You have family here?"

"My name's Danny Fortune, and this is my friend Courtney Johnson. We're looking for my father."

"Sorry I can't get up," Bates whispered.

Courtney had never seen anything like this. She stood there quietly as Danny made conversation with the wounded young soldier. He was lying on a filthy blanket, and the bandage around his head was dirty and needed changing. Courtney couldn't help but think about her closet at home, bursting with clothes that she hadn't worn more than once. His eyes returned to her, and she knew she had to say something. "If we had known we were coming, we would have brought you something." Then a thought came to her. "Wait, I do have something, Danny. You remember we packed the lunches, and we didn't eat nearly all of it."

"Oh, thank you, miss, but I can't keep anything down."

This silenced Courtney, and she stood there uncomfortably, not having any idea what she should say.

Danny talked to the soldier for a while longer until Colonel Hamilton suddenly appeared. "When you two are ready, we can leave."

"I hope you get better, Nathaniel," Danny said.

"So do I," Courtney added.

Nathaniel Bates nodded slightly, then closed his eyes and seemed to pass into unconsciousness at once. They walked down the hall and thanked Dr.

Simmons. Danny stopped long enough to ask, "Will Nathaniel get well?"

Dr. Simmons' face grew almost angry. "If he had proper care he might. But no. He's going to die. There's nothing more I can do for him."

A cold shock ran through Courtney. *He's not much older than me, and he's going to die.* She had never had to deal with death before, and now she stood there feeling helpless.

6

Finding the location of a single man in the Continental Army of the United States should have been simple—or so Danny had thought. But Lieutenant Masters, the quartermaster of the army, had said with some discouragement, "We left all of our records back in New York, and they've never been restored since. Men come and go. Sometimes their names never find their way onto our rolls, and many, of course, have deserted."

"We'll just have to hang around for a while, Courtney, and hope that Lieutenant Masters will find my dad."

Danny was sitting on a log outside the shabby hut that he and Courtney were staying in. There had not been enough room to house them individually, so they were both put in the cook's quarters. Danny glanced over at Courtney, who was sitting across from him on an upturned wooden bucket.

Courtney's face was set in a frown, and she shook her head. "We'll never find your dad, Danny, and I don't think I can live in this horrible place much longer."

Valley Forge was a terrible place. Dreary and unwelcoming—an almost deserted valley beneath lines of wooded hills. The British had already scoured Valley Forge the previous September for supplies, stripping it bare. Some they had paid for, and some they had simply carried off.

The inhabitants were not all in favor of the Revolution. Many of them were firm Loyalists to King George III and the British Empire. They refused to sell food or livestock to the quartermaster because they did not accept Continental money, which had become almost worthless.

Danny had explained to Courtney, "Continental money was printed without anything to back it up, so it was just like Monopoly money."

Courtney glanced around over the bleak, gray hillsides that surrounded the camp. Everywhere greenwood fires sent long columns of gray smoke into the air as the weary, hungry, and freezing men huddled around them.

As they sat there, their stomachs growled with hunger. They had brought little food with them from the inn and had survived on that, but they knew that the soldiers had almost nothing. Every night a cry went through the camp, "No meat! No meat!"

A butcher had brought a quarter of poor, stringy beef into the camp that afternoon, and a soldier had said, "Look at that skinny piece of meat! There's more to eat on my buttons than there is on that thing!"

Colonel Hamilton had invited Danny and

Courtney to dine with the officers once, and they'd eaten food that they would have turned down at home. There was soggy fire-cake, bread baked over a fire, and some stringy beef that both of them had a hard time chewing. During the meal Danny wished with all his heart that he could encourage the officers, who were all hungry and discouraged, about their Revolution. *Don't worry, you guys. You're going to win this war. You're building a great country here. Don't give up!*

Now as Danny sat looking across the camp, he was surprised when Courtney said abruptly, "Let's go back home, Danny."

"Back home? We can't do that."

"Why not? If we stay here we could starve to death. I'm cold, I haven't had a shower since yesterday morning, and bugs are eating me alive. Bed bugs, I think they are. Next thing you know I'll have lice in my hair, and I'll have to cut it all off."

Danny got up and walked over to sit beside Courtney. "I know it's rough," he said in a comforting tone, "but I told you it would be."

"You didn't tell me what it would smell like," Courtney shot back.

"The men can't help it that they haven't been able to take a bath." Danny was beginning to get irritated with her. Couldn't she at least try to understand?

Courtney pulled her wool cap off and began to scratch her head. "My head itches so bad from not being able to wash it, and look at my hands." Her fingernails were ragged where she had bitten them off. "I must look terrible. I want to go home right now!"

Danny was struggling between his feelings of being furious at Courtney for her attitude and just wanting to be near her because he liked her so much. He swallowed hard and shook his head stubbornly. "We're not going, and that's all there is to it!"

Courtney suddenly reached out and slapped Danny on the cheek. "You've got to take me home! You dragged me here! If you don't take me back, I'm going to die in this place!"

Danny's face burned beneath the blow, even though it wasn't very hard. He saw that Courtney was afraid and angry—but above all, she was spoiled. He gritted his teeth and shook his head again. "We're not going home without my dad, or at least until we've done all we can to find him." He got up and left Courtney sitting on the bucket, her face steaming with anger.

As he walked away, his feet numb and his lips stiff from the intense cold, he kept an eye on every man he passed. If he saw someone he hadn't spoken to yet, he'd ask if they had heard of a James Fortune. By this time, though, he had already seen most of the men in the camp. His only hope now was that his father was off serving with a unit in some other part of the Colonies. There were other units—some serving with General Gates, who had joined the Colonial cause and was commander of the troops in the Carolinas.

Danny was beginning to think he should go down

south to the Carolinas to see if he could find his dad there. But there were still several units closer under Washington's command, and he decided stubbornly that he would stay.

Courtney was more miserable than she had ever imagined she could be. After slapping Danny, things became even worse. For the first time in her life, she felt guilty, although she had a hard time admitting it to herself. Courtney didn't have much practice at saying she was sorry. By spoiling her, Courtney's parents had unknowingly given her the idea that it was up to everyone else to apologize to *her*.

After Danny left, she got up and walked miserably back and forth for a while. Her mind whirling, she tried to think of a way to force Danny to take her home.

I know he likes me a lot, she thought. *If only we were back home I'd know what to do. I could smile at him and pay attention to him and let him take me places—then I'd get what I wanted. But I can't do that out here.* She looked down at the ugly boots that covered her feet, the thick, gray wool of her dress, and suddenly she felt as alone as she ever had in her life.

Still pacing, she went over the argument she had had with Danny. She waited for about half an hour, hoping he would come back, but he did not. She went inside the cold hut they were sharing with the cook and wrapped up in all the blankets she could find, trying to keep warm. With nothing else to do, she shivered as she tried to go to sleep.

Moments later, she heard a knock at the door. It startled her, and she quickly got up from the rough cot. A bitter smile touched her lips as she smoothed her hair down. She thought of how dirty and stringy it had gotten. Opening the door she found a short, rather heavyset man standing there dressed in a uniform of sorts.

"Yes? What is it?" she asked.

"Are you Miss Fortune?"

"No. My name is Courtney Johnson. Are you looking for Danny Fortune?"

"Ah yes. That's the name. Is he here?"

"No, sir. He's gone. He should be back soon, though."

"My name is Efriam Tanner, and I'm happy to know you." He hesitated for a moment before saying, "I understand that you two are looking for Mr. Fortune's father."

"Yes," Courtney replied eagerly. "Do you know him?"

"Well, I'm not certain."

Courtney peered at him and asked, "Are you a soldier?"

Tanner smiled and shook his head regretfully. "I guess I'd say I'm part soldier and part preacher. I'm a chaplain with his Excellency's Continental Army."

Eager to find any news at all of Danny's father so

that she could get back to her own life, Courtney said, "Please come in out of the cold, Reverend. We can build a fire and get warm."

"Well, if you think he won't be long." The minister walked inside the small hut, which was no more than ten feet square, and looked at the fireplace made of mud and sticks. "Perhaps I could build that fire for you. I'm very good at it."

"That would be great—if you don't mind." Courtney had had no success at all building fires. It required a skill that she had never practiced. She watched as Reverend Tanner quickly assembled some small sticks and pulled portions of rags and dried bark from his pocket. "I always carry these with me," he said. "It makes it much easier." He got a small pile made, took out a pouch, and covered it with black powder, then removed a piece of steel and flint from his inner pocket.

Courtney watched with interest as he held the flint and struck it with a piece of steel. After three tries a tiny spark fell on the powder, which ignited at once, and Reverend Tanner exclaimed, "Ahh, that does it!" He nursed the fire carefully, speaking of the cold weather and the hard conditions of the army.

Courtney drew near the fire as it began to blaze and put her hands out to it, soaking up the warmth. It made a cheerful sound in the gloom of the hut, which had been dimly lit by one stub of a candle. "Thank you for building the fire, Reverend Tanner."

"Nothing at all! Nothing at all, Miss Courtney!"

"Here, sit down. I wish there were something we could eat or drink, but I'm afraid—"

"That's quite all right. Supplies are scarce. I'd like to hear about you, though. I've been with the troops down in the south, and I heard from Colonel Hamilton only this morning about your friend's search for his father. Would you care to tell me more about it?"

Courtney and Danny had perfected a story about how they happened to come to the camp, and she told it quickly. "I hope you can help him. Mr. Fortune really needs to be back at home. His family needs him."

This was one thing that Courtney had learned. She had known almost nothing of Danny's home life, and as they had spent hours together she discovered he had a sick brother that required expensive treatments. She also learned that because his mother worked all day, Danny and Dixie did much of the housework, as well as cared for Jimmy. She felt a little ashamed that she hadn't really known or cared about how hard a life Danny had, and now she said, "We can't stay at Valley Forge forever, and it would be so good if you could help us find Mr. Fortune."

At that moment there were footsteps outside, then the door opened as Danny entered.

Courtney jumped up in excitement. "Danny," she exclaimed, "this is Reverend Efriam Tanner. He came by with some news about your father."

Tanner shook his head at once as he rose. "Uh,

nothing that definite, I'm afraid. I'm glad to meet you, young man."

Danny's face lit up with hope. "Do you know my father? His name is James Fortune."

"I seem to remember the name, but I meet so many men, you understand. I've just come back from General Gates's command, and before that I was with General Washington during the first year of the war. I've met thousands of men."

"But did you ever know one named Fortune?"

Reverend Tanner stroked his jaw thoughtfully. "I'm almost positive that I did. It's such an unusual name—Fortune. I'm certain I've heard it somewhere." His gray eyes saw how anxious Danny looked, and he told him gently, "I'm sure it will come to me. If I try to force it, I can't think of it. But if I leave it alone, then sometimes it just pops into my mind. Maybe in the middle of the night. I'm dreadfully sorry," he said. "I wish I had better news."

"We're very grateful to you, sir." Danny tried to look happy, but his face showed how discouraged he was.

Reverend Tanner hesitated. "Perhaps it would be good if we were to put this before God."

"Yes," Danny agreed eagerly. "Would you pray for us, and for my father, wherever he is?"

"Are you two Christians?"

Danny nodded at once, but Courtney made no move whatsoever. She felt the eyes of the short chaplain on her face and then heard him say, "Miss

Courtney, it is a comforting thing to know Jesus as your personal savior. As I pray for Danny's father to be found, would it be all right if I pray for you as well?"

Courtney had never been so embarrassed before. She did not understand what the chaplain meant. The idea of a "personal savior" was something she had never understood. She hesitated for a long moment, aware that Danny and the chaplain were both waiting for her to reply. Finally, out of politeness, she murmured, "I suppose it would be all right." She dropped her eyes, and the chaplain began to pray.

As Reverend Tanner finished his prayer, Danny stole a glance at Courtney and saw that her face was pale.

Courtney was feeling absolutely miserable. As the other two watched her, she could not meet their eyes. She had always avoided kids her own age who were Christians, and now she felt trapped. Even so, there was something in the words of the preacher that had stirred her heart.

Danny, not wanting Courtney to be embarrassed further, quickly came to her rescue. "Thank you very much for stopping by, Reverend Tanner, and for your prayers."

"I'll be ministering to the troops this evening. I wish both of you would come to the service."

"I'll be there," Danny said. He glanced at Courtney, who didn't make a sound, then shook the chaplain's hand. "I look forward to hearing your sermon."

"I know God will be with both of you and trust that you will find your heart's desire." Tanner shook hands with Danny and bowed low to Courtney.

"Well," Danny said after the door closed, "that's something, isn't it? He goes everywhere. Now that he knows Dad's name, he'll be able to help."

"I hope so. Anything to get out of this place." Courtney went over and sat down on her cot, clasped her hands together, and stared at the floor. She wanted to apologize to Danny for the way she had acted, but pride stood in her way. And now she was troubled at the thought of what the chaplain had said about letting Jesus come into her heart.

Danny tried to be cheerful. "I got some dried berries from an old woman who lives about a mile from here." He reached and picked up a sack that he had brought inside with him and put one of the berries in his mouth. "Hmmm, not bad. Not as good as fresh strawberries, but they're edible." He held out the sack and watched as Courtney slowly reached out and took one. He could tell she was deep in thought, and he knew somehow that the preacher's words had gotten to her. He said another little prayer as they sat there— not only for his father, but also for Courtney to find Jesus.

7

Danny was growing discouraged. He had discovered that his father was not with any of the units settled in Valley Forge, and the scouts that stayed on the outskirts of the army camp had all come in, but none of them had ever heard of a James Fortune. Maybe it was the lack of food and the terrible conditions that drained him, but by the end of the second week he had almost given up hope.

On a Thursday morning he got up early and wandered down the lines of log huts. He walked with his head down for the most part, kicking at the chunks of ice that had been formed from soldiers packing down the snow as they marched on it. From far away came the cry of a coyote. He reached the end of the camp and walked over to the line of trees, trying hard to think of what to do. He had only been there a few minutes when a movement to his left caught his eye. He turned to see a tall officer walking out of the woods, and he recognized General Washington as he drew closer.

The general looked up quickly and nodded, saying, "Well, young man, how are you this morning?"

"I'm fine, General Washington."

"A good breakfast wouldn't go bad, would it?" Washington was wearing a blue coat over his uniform, fastened together at the throat. He was not wearing gloves, and his large hands seemed to be numb. "I wish every soldier in the army could have a good breakfast this morning."

"I wish that, too, General." Once again, Danny longed to tell the general that this was the worst of it for the Continental Army. Desertions had robbed Washington of many of his men, and now it seemed as if the Revolution that had begun so strong was falling apart. But he knew he must keep silent. "It'll be spring soon, General Washington. I'm sure many of the men who couldn't take this cold weather will come back again."

"That's my prayer," General Washington nodded. "It's hard to ask men to leave their families and endure such hardships. Sometimes I think I'm asking too much of them."

"They love you, sir," Danny said. "They wouldn't follow any other man in the Colonies as they've followed you."

"I'm not certain about that," Washington murmured, his voice low. He turned his eyes back to Danny. "What will you do? Go back to your home?"

"I thought about going south to see if my father's with General Gates's forces."

"Well, the weather would be milder there. I certainly hope you find him, son." Washington smiled more fully, put out his hand, and closed it around Danny's. Then the general walked away, his shoulders seeming to sag with discouragement.

Somehow the meeting with General Washington had encouraged Danny, and he went back to find Courtney. But when he got there he discovered that the hut was empty. "She's probably gone to the hospital," he muttered as he built up the fire. "I know she's been there at least once to see Bates."

Courtney had gone to the hospital. When she had awakened and found Danny missing, she ate some of the dried, hard beef that was all they had left and melted some snow over the fire to get fresh water. After that she had moved restlessly around the hut, but it was too cramped. She had not slept well and muttered to herself, "I might as well go to the hospital and see Nathaniel. At least I'll be doing some good that way."

Leaving the hut, she made her way to the hospital, and when she arrived she found Dr. Simmons sitting inside at the small desk, writing.

"Well, good morning, miss. Have you come to visit with my patients?"

"Yes, I have, Doctor Simmons."

He nodded. "It'll be good for them. Poor fellows. Most of them will never live to see the spring."

The doctor's words saddened Courtney, but she remembered why she had come. "I'd like to see Nathaniel."

"That'll be good," Simmons nodded. "He sleeps most of the time. It's more of a coma than a sleep, but you go see him. Try to cheer him up."

Moving down the ranks of wounded men, Courtney nodded and tried to smile at several of them. They were in such terrible condition. She had always thought of a hospital as a place where people got better; a place with shiny tiled floors, spotless walls, and filled with all sorts of equipment. Now, as she moved along and looked at the dirt floor and the filthy blankets the men wrapped themselves in, a heaviness fell over her.

When she reached the little alcove Nathaniel was sharing with three other men, she moved over to his cot. There was nothing to sit on, so she knelt down and whispered, "Nathaniel, are you awake?"

The wounded boy's eyes opened slowly, and a smile touched his lips that were blue from the cold.

"Hello . . . Courtney." His voice was barely a whisper as he tried to speak.

"How do you feel?"

"I don't complain."

"No, you never do," Courtney agreed. "Oh, I wish I had something good for you to eat."

"I'm not very hungry."

"What does the doctor say about your wound?"

"Oh, the doctor don't say much. I think he's given up on me." His eyes were almost closed, and his whisper was hard to hear. "I've about given up on myself, I reckon."

Impulsively, Courtney reached out and took the thin hand. She squeezed it with both of hers. "You mustn't do that, Nathaniel."

Nathaniel opened his eyes and there was surprise in them. "Why, I've seen so many of our men die. I guess I've gotten used to it. Don't seem so bad now." There was a silence, and he held on to her hand. Then he squeezed it harder as he said, "Are you afraid of death, Miss Courtney?"

"Yes, I am," Courtney admitted.

"Well, I used to be. I guess the Reverend Tanner—he's helped me a lot. He prayed with me, you know, and I asked the Lord Jesus to take over my life. And He did."

"Did He, Nathaniel?" Courtney leaned closer and brushed a lock of hair out of the young man's eyes. "What was it like?"

"Well, it didn't seem like much at first. He just told me to ask Jesus to forgive my sins, and I done that. Then he told me to ask Him to just come and live inside me, and I done that."

"Did you feel any different?"

"Well, not right off. But you know, it's peculiar, Miss Courtney. Ever since that time I been gettin' more and more—well, *peaceful*, I guess you might say. I'd like to live and see my folks again . . . but if I don't, well, that's all right, too."

Courtney sat there in the cold room, kneeling on

the dirt floor. She stayed for a while, just keeping Nathaniel company.

"I sure thank you for comin' to visit with me," Nathaniel whispered. "It's meant a lot to me and the other fellas here."

Courtney's eyes welled up with tears, and she blinked them away. "It's . . . it's the least I can do."

"No, it ain't. It's a lot to do. Not many fine, young women like you would come into a filthy place like this with all these dirty, dying men. It ain't a little thing," he insisted. He smiled again, then weariness seemed to overcome him, and his eyes closed slowly.

Getting to her feet, Courtney made her way out of the hospital, only subconsiously hearing the doctor say, "Come back again, miss."

When she was outside, the cold bit into her face, and she drew the cloak around her as she began walking back to the hut. Several of the soldiers she passed looked at her with curiosity. One of them said, "Shore seems funny to see a pretty, young human being, don't it, Ed?"

"Shore does!"

As she walked along and thought of Nathaniel, she recalled how the reverend had prayed for Danny's father. *Is that what I should do? Pray for Nathaniel?* She had heard prayers in church, but somehow they did not seem to be what she needed. In desperation, she cried out within her heart, *Oh, God, I don't know how to talk to you, but I want you to help Nathaniel. I'll do anything if you'll just tell me.*

Moving across the packed snow, an idea began to take form in her mind. She wondered if her prayers could really be answered that quickly. Whatever it was, by the time she got back to the hut, her mind was made up.

⚡ ⚡ ⚡

Danny was returning to the hut, carrying some sticks from the woods, when he heard Courtney call to him, "Come inside. I've got to talk to you."

When they were inside, Danny put the sticks down, then turned to face Courtney. He saw a determined light in her blue eyes, and her lips were drawn together with purpose. "What is it, Courtney?" he asked quickly. He thought she was going to demand that he take her home again and was surprised at what she said.

"We've got to help those men in the hospital—especially Nathaniel Bates."

"Help him? How can we do that?"

"How many of those coins do you have left?"

Danny stared at her, wondering what was on her mind. Reaching into his pocket, he pulled them out and held them in his palm. "It looks like seven. Why do you want to know?"

"Because we're going to go into that little town where we bought the horse and buggy. They've got food there, and medicine and soap. We're going to save Nathaniel Bates."

"Well, I don't know about that. The doctor doesn't hold out much hope for him."

For one instant Courtney hesitated, then she decided to tell Danny what had happened. "I don't know what it means," she said slowly, "but on my way back here, I couldn't think of anything but Nathaniel. And, Danny . . . I prayed. The first time in my life, almost."

"What did you pray about?"

"I asked God to help Nathaniel, and I told Him I'd do anything I could. And you know what?" Courtney's eyes grew soft. "I don't know whether it was God or not, but as soon as I had prayed that, I had this idea. I think it's something we've got to do."

"Well, if you think God's told us to go get supplies, then we'll do it."

"Will you, Danny?" Danny was surprised when Courtney moved closer and took his hand. "Would you really do that?"

For months Danny had dreamed of holding Courtney Johnson's hand, but he had never once thought it would take place in a dirty hut in Valley Forge, where the Continental Army of the United States was suffering its most terrible time.

He squeezed her hand, then a smile came to his lips. "I'm glad you prayed, and I think God is answering. So let's go to the village and get those supplies."

8

George Washington sat at his desk, his shoulders stooped and his head half bowed, his mind struggling with the almost unsolvable problems of this Revolution. He thought of Benjamin Franklin's words after they had agreed to pull away from England. "We must all hang together now, or we will all hang separately." But they were not hanging together. Men were deserting while on guard duty and disobeying orders by gambling. Quartermasters were embezzling clothing and flour to be sold in Philadelphia while his army starved. And to add to his troubles, he was enduring an attack from General Gates, who had a desperate desire to be Commander in Chief of the Confederate forces. Others joined with Gates, and Washington, who was admittedly the idol of America, had to fight within the ranks of the army, as well as with the British.

Washington stood and moved over to the single window in his small office, staring out at the scarecrow figures of his soldiers. *With these men*, he thought, *I have to win a war against the finest troops in Europe*. The thought seemed to depress him, and he turned again to his desk. A knock at the door caught his attention, and his aide announced, "Someone to see you, General."

"Who is it?"

"The two visitors—Fortune and the young woman."

"Have them come in," Washington said, surprise filling his voice. When Danny and Courtney entered, he quickly said, "I expected you to be gone to the south."

"I thought so, too, General. But there's one thing we need to do," Danny replied. He motioned to Courtney. "Miss Johnson has been visiting the hospital. She's very concerned about one of the soldiers— about all of them, of course—but one in particular. His name is Nathaniel Bates."

"I don't believe I know that name."

"He's going to die if he doesn't get help, General Washington," Danny said.

"I'm afraid that's true of many of our wounded."

"General, would you give us a pass to go into town and come back?" Courtney asked.

"Why, whatever for, Miss Johnson?"

"We have some money—Danny and I—some gold coins. We want to go in and buy what food and medicine we can and take care of Nathaniel and as many of the others as possible."

A look of surprise swept across Washington's ragged face. "That is most kind of you both," he said, "and certainly I will give you a pass." He moved to his desk, scribbled out a few words on a sheet of paper, then extended it to Danny. "This will get you out of camp and back again." He hesitated, then added sorrowfully, "I only wish more of our people would help as you are offering to do."

"Many would, General," Danny said quickly, "if they were here and saw what was going on."

"I'm sure you're right, my boy. Well, I can only give you the thanks of an old soldier, and I will never forget you for this."

Danny and Courtney said at the same time, "Thank you, General." They turned and left the office and went at once to the stable where the officers' horses were kept. A corporal met them, and Danny asked for help in harnessing his horse to the buggy. When that was done, they got in and left quickly.

"At least this is one good that'll come out of this trip—even if we don't find my dad."

Courtney leaned over and pressed her shoulder against his. "Don't give up hope, Danny. Maybe something will turn up soon."

It was the first encouraging thing Courtney Johnson had said. *She's changing. She hasn't even said anything about going home for the last twenty-four hours.*

Robert Benson, the owner of the small store where Danny had bought the supplies earlier, looked up with surprise.

"Well, here you are again!"

"Yes, sir. We want to buy some food and medicine, if you have them, and some good blankets." Danny slipped his hand into his pocket, pulled out the leather pouch, and jangled the remaining gold coins. He saw Benson's eyes brighten. "We've got to get as much as we can, Mr. Benson, but you've got to give us good prices."

"For gold? I'll certainly do that, my boy. Now, let's see. Do you have a list?"

Danny and Courtney hurried up the steps to Dr. Simmons' cabin and knocked loudly on the door.

The doctor opened the door and peeked out, looking worn and exhausted. Danny figured he had been up all night with the dying soldiers. "Is something wrong? Is there a problem with one of the men?"

"No, there's nothing wrong," Courtney said at once. "We've brought food and medicine and blankets for the men. They're out here in the wagon."

"Supplies . . . medicine?" Dr. Simmons rushed outside and saw the wagon piled high with supplies and covered with a canvas tarp. Ignoring the cold, he hurried over to the wagon and pulled back the tarp, his eyes gleaming. His voice came alive as he said, "Why, bless my soul!" He turned to Danny and Courtney. "How did you accomplish this?"

"Well," Danny winked at Courtney, "I think God

had something to do with it."

The physician blinked with surprise. "Well, thank God for His mercies. Now then, let's see what you have here."

🔆 🔆 🔆

Nathaniel Bates was looking very much alive. He had been washed with carbolic soap by Danny, he was wearing clean bedclothes, and a thick, wool blanket was tucked under his legs. Now, propped up in the bed, he was actually eating a bowl of hot soup.

Courtney watched him with a smile. "Is it good?"

"Good, miss? Why, I reckon it's the best food I ever had in my whole life." He took another swallow of the soup, then a bite of the freshly baked bread. He looked around at his three friends, who were all covered with fresh blankets and eating from the iron pot of soup that Courtney had brought in.

"Don't rightly seem real." Nathaniel Bates shook his head. "Reckon when you came with all them clothes and all that medicine and this good food, why, I thought it was an angel come from heaven."

Courtney blushed, then shook her head at once. "Don't say that, Nathaniel. I'm not anything like an angel."

"Well, I'm callin' you one."

A tall, lanky man across from Nathaniel nodded. His name was David Baines, and he was from Virginia. "An angel couldn't look no better than you, Miss

Courtney, and we all thank you for it."

Courtney sat there, her face warm with the praise of the soldiers. She took the bowls after they were finished and instructed, "Try to get some sleep now. Did you all take the medicine the doctor gave you?"

"Yes, ma'am, we did," Nathaniel said. He reached out his hand suddenly, and when Courtney took it, he enclosed it with both of his. With surprising strength, he said, "Maybe you're not an angel, but I'll always think of you that way, Miss Courtney. God surely sent you."

A strange feeling coursed through Courtney. She had been paid many compliments in her life, but this one truly meant something to her. She knew that for the rest of her life she would always remember this moment.

Courtney went to find Danny, who was bringing a pot of tea down the line, pouring it for the men, along with some fresh bread and cakes. He looked up at her. "How is Nathaniel?"

"Much better. I think he has a chance now."

When they finally left the hospital, Courtney was tired. It had been a long trip to town, and she was slow to get into the wagon. They had been forced to trade the buggy for a wagon in order to carry the supplies, and the seat was hard.

Danny said nothing until the horse started up. Finally he looked at her and said, "You sure have changed, Courtney."

With a startled look, Courtney met his eyes. "What do you mean?"

Danny was thoughtful for a moment, then said, "Well, the old Courtney Johnson I knew wouldn't have come up with an idea like this." Danny didn't say anything more than that. He didn't want to hurt Courtney's feelings.

When they got to their shabby hut, the cook was already asleep in the corner. Danny went over to warm his hands by the dwindling fire. He thought hard about the last couple of days and how much they had been through. "Courtney," he whispered, "you've been through a lot here. If you want me to, I'll take you back to our time, then I'll return by myself." He fully expected Courtney to jump at the chance but was surprised when she shook her head.

"No, I'll stay as long as you want to, Danny."

Danny stared at her, then shook his head and reached out and touched her cheek. "You don't know how much it means to me to hear you say that, Courtney!"

9

Dixie sat in her beanbag chair, looking up at the television set, bored out of her skull. "I wish I'd gone to school today," she muttered rebelliously. "And I wish *I* could have gone with Danny to look for Dad."

Since getting the phone call from her Uncle Mordecai about Danny's whereabouts, Dixie was a little upset that Danny hadn't waited for her. On top of that, she was even more upset that he had taken Courtney Johnson with him. What would she know about getting their dad back?

Rolling out of the beanbag, she stood upright and put her hand on her forehead. "Doesn't feel like much of a temperature to me," she muttered. Her mother had been concerned enough about her to insist that she stay home from school. Jimmy had gone to a baby-sitter for the day, and now Dixie wandered around the apartment all morning, occasionally staring blankly at the television.

Moving into the kitchen, she poured herself a bowl of Cheerios, put in two heaping spoonfuls of sugar, then drowned it in milk. Her forehead was wrinkled in a frown, and she thought again about Danny and

Courtney. "I should never have let Danny go off without me. He needs a backup, and Courtney is *not* the person for that job."

She ate half the bowl of cereal, then gave up and poured it down the sink. Flipping the switch for the garbage disposal, she watched with satisfaction as the little O's were sucked down into the grinder.

She wandered back in front of the television and watched with disgust. "Nothing but garbage on," she muttered and shut it off.

Dixie stretched, then went over to look out the window. As always, when she grew still she thought of her father and how much different it was when he had been home. A sadness came over her, and she fought back the thought, *We'll never find him! Not ever!*

She walked across the room to where a small desk was set in the corner. It was her father's desk, an antique built of rosewood by some skilled woodworker maybe a hundred years ago. Running her hand over the satiny wood, she thought of how many times she had seen her father sit at this desk doing his work. A lump came to her throat, and she had trouble swallowing.

Sitting down in the chair, she pulled open the drawer and sifted through the three notebooks that were there. She, Danny, and their mother had gone through all of them, hoping one would contain a clue about their father's disappearance. But they found nothing.

Idly she pulled the drawer out farther to get at the

little bundle of notes that was in the back, although she knew she would find nothing there, either. A fire truck siren suddenly burst into a loud scream just outside the apartment building, causing her to jump. As she did so, she pulled the drawer completely out and looked down in dismay as the contents were scattered all over the floor.

"Oh no!" Getting down on her hands and knees, Dixie began to gather the papers, notebooks, paper clips, and ball-point pens. She turned to the drawer, which had fallen in an upside-down position, intending to flip it over and put the contents back in. But she froze when she saw a sheet of folded paper taped to the underside of the drawer.

With a trembling hand, she reached out and carefully removed the tape, and when she unfolded the paper she saw that there was a single message in her father's handwriting. Her heart leaped as she scanned the words.

I'm going to go back to do research for Mordecai and Zacharias. My destination will be Valley Forge. That was, I think, when this country was really saved. If Washington had given up then, or if the army had been allowed to disappear, the Revolution would have been lost, and we would have been British subjects.

I'll go back not as James Fortune but as James Dare. That was my mother's maiden name, and I feel inclined to use it on this trip. So I, James Dare, will go back and witness the darkest hour of the American Revolution.

Dixie stared at the note in disbelief, then suddenly it all made sense. "Oh no, if Danny is there looking for James Fortune, he'll never find him. Nobody would have ever heard of him!"

The sound of the siren was disappearing down the street in a frail, tiny, wailing sound. Dixie's mind was racing furiously. "I've got to get to Danny somehow."

Instantly she began to devise a plan, and after grabbing her coat, she raced out the front door. She thought once about leaving a note, but decided not to. *I'll just go to Zacharias's and Mordecai's. They can send me back to help Danny find Dad under his new name. We could be back in no time.*

As she raced down the street, she saw a yellow cab coming toward her. It was empty, and she waved her arms frantically. When it stopped, she got in the back and gave the directions. "And hurry, please!"

"All right, miss." The cabby threw the flag down, and Dixie sat back, watching the numbers advance on the meter. Her mind was spinning with what she had found, and she suddenly remembered that she had been praying for some way to find her father. "Maybe this is an answer to my prayer," she murmured under her breath.

When the cab got to the old mansion, she paid the

driver, and he asked if he should wait for her.

"No. But if you could give me your company's phone number, I'll call you when I'm ready to go home." She took the card that the cab driver handed her and waved as he took off down the road.

Wheeling around, Dixie ran up the steps. She knocked on the door, and almost at once Toombs opened it. He glared at her with his small, piggish eyes. Toombs always seemed irritated when anyone came. "What do you want?"

"I have to see my uncles."

"They're busy."

"I have to see them now, Toombs. Please!"

Toombs hesitated. He made a grim shape in the doorway, and for a moment Dixie thought he was going to slam the door in her face. Instead, he shrugged his beefy shoulders and opened the door a little wider, stepping back. "You wait in the foyer," he warned.

As he disappeared down the hall, Dixie began rehearsing her story. Her uncles could be very stubborn, and she hoped this would not be one of those days.

Five minutes later, Toombs came lumbering back down the hall. "Your uncles will see you."

"Oh, thank you, Toombs."

Running down the long hallway, Dixie took the stairway that led to the laboratory and found her uncles waiting for her.

"What is it?" Mordecai demanded. "We don't have time to chat."

"You've got to read this note," Dixie said, knowing

that an explanation would take too long.

Mordecai glared at her and snatched the note. He ran his sharp, black eyes over it and instantly grasped what it meant. "Look at this, Zacharias. James is using another name. Danny and that girl will never find him. They're looking for James Fortune."

"Why in the world did he have to change his name? It just makes everything more difficult!" Zacharias exclaimed angrily. He ran his hand through his white hair. "Well, we'll just have to wait until they come back, then try it all over again."

"No," Dixie said. "That won't do."

"What do you mean it won't do?" Zacharias questioned her.

"I don't want Danny to waste any more time there than he has to. It's not safe. Without knowing what name Dad is really using, he's on a wild goose chase. I've got to get to him right now!"

"There's no way to get to him."

"Yes, there is." Dixie had thought all this out. "Send me to the same place you sent Danny, and I'll find him."

"You might never find him. We have only one reliable Recall Unit, and Danny has it. If you don't find him, you'd be lost just like your father."

"We've got to do it!" Dixie pleaded. "After all, it's just a matter of finding Valley Forge and the army camp. We know that's where they were going."

"We don't know that. A hundred things might have

happened. They might have gotten lost. It would be too dangerous."

Dixie talked as fast as she could, quickly giving reasons for why this was so urgent. Finally Zacharias threw his hands up. "All right. We'll let you go. But if anything happens to you, we're not to blame."

Mordecai was alarmed at his brother's statement. "I'm not sure about this, Zacharias."

"It'll be all right, Mordecai. She has a point, you know. She'll find them, and he'll get the message. Somehow I just feel that this is going to work."

Mordecai required more persuasion, but finally he exclaimed, "Well, if you want to take the risk, it's on your own head!"

Dixie ran over and hugged Mordecai, then turned to Zacharias and hugged him also. "Oh, it's going to work! I just know it is. Let's start right now."

Dixie hurried to the Chrono-Shuttle, but Zacharias stopped her. "Just a minute. You'll freeze to death without a coat, and people in that time wouldn't know what to think about a girl wearing pants."

Finding Dixie an appropriate outfit took another twenty minutes. The uncles had accumulated quite a few costumes to fit the twins under different conditions, and finally Dixie stood there before the shuttle, wearing a pair of light brown boots, a gray dress that came down to the tops of them, and a heavy, brown woolen coat. A wool hat that covered her ears finished the costume. "I'm burning up in this," Dixie complained.

"You won't be when you get to Valley Forge," Mordecai said grimly. "Here's some gold coins to get you by. . . . Well, let's get on with it."

Dixie climbed into the Chrono-Shuttle. It was the first time she had ever gotten into it alone, and she began to shiver with nervousness. She said nothing to her uncles, however, but began to pray. *Lord, just get me there and help me to find Danny and Courtney.*

Zacharias walked over and began to move his hands across the control panel. Dixie felt the vibration of the Chrono-Shuttle, and the air seemed to be turning a light, pale green. "I'm going!" she cried out. "I'll be back with the others!" Then the Chrono-Shuttle dissolved, and Dixie along with it.

10

"Oooh! I didn't know it would be so cold!"

Dixie's first sensation was the biting, bitter cold that seemed to go right through her clothing and chill her bones. She had found herself, as always, lying flat on her back. As she got up and dusted the snow from the back of her coat, she shivered and looked around at the huge oaks and hickories that surrounded her.

"It's a good thing I didn't wind up hanging from a tree," she said aloud, breaking the silence of the muted winter day.

Turning around, she looked for a road, a house, a farm, or *something* resembling civilization—but all she saw was a clearing in the trees over to her right. The skirt of her dress dragged through the snow as she waded through it, clumps of ice clinging to the wool. When she made her way out of the woods, she found herself on a road that seemed to be fairly well traveled. Hesitating for a moment, not knowing whether to go to her right or left, she shrugged and turned to her right. *Not many people lived around here in these days*, she thought as she went along. *I might have to walk ten miles before I find a village or a house.*

Fortunately, Dixie had not traveled more than twenty minutes when she saw a house set back off the road about fifty feet. Smoke was curling up out of the cabin, and she eagerly trudged on until she came up to the front steps. A huge black dog came sailing around the side of the house, barking fiercely.

"Nice dog," Dixie called and tried to conceal her fear. The dog stopped, bared his fangs, and kept his head low. "You're a *very* nice dog," Dixie said with encouragement. She stuck her hand out, and he growled even more fiercely. She pulled her hand back quickly. At that moment the door opened, and Dixie turned quickly to see an old woman step out onto the porch. She was small and had a wrinkled face like an old apple and was bent over with age.

"Hello, ma'am," Dixie said quickly. "Does this dog bite?"

"Sometimes." The old woman's eyes were sharp, despite her age. "Where's a young thing like you goin' in the dead of winter? You're liable to freeze your toes off."

"I'm looking for General Washington's camp at Valley Forge."

"Well, come on in the house. I'll feed you some stew."

"Well, I really need to be on my—"

But the old woman had turned and walked into the house. Dixie followed her at once, thinking it might be easier. When she was inside, her eyes swept the cabin, which was only one room with a ladder leading up to a loft. A huge stone fireplace took up one entire end of the cabin. The old woman moved over and, picking up a bowl, spooned out some thick-looking stew. Returning, she set it down on the table and fished a wooden spoon from her apron.

Thinking she might not be able to eat again for some time, Dixie sat down and was surprised to find the stew very good. She decided to be brave and ask what was in it.

"Everything I had on the place. A little squirrel, a little possum, a little coon. I call it my little-bit-of-everything stew."

Dixie froze, holding the spoon in her mouth for a few seconds. She was having a hard time swallowing the bite she had just taken and was on the verge of spitting it out. She tried her hardest to ignore the ingredients and instead concentrate on the fact that she was hungry and would probably need to fill her stomach for the journey ahead. With all the courage she could muster, she swallowed what was in her mouth.

"What you goin' to them army fellers for?" the old woman asked.

"I'm looking for my father. I think he's in the army there."

"Well, you ain't too fer from it. Wagons come along pretty quick. It's about ten miles down this here road, then you leave and take another four miles down into the valley."

Dixie's heart lifted. She knew she could walk that far if she had to. She finished the stew and downed a long drink of water from a cup that the elderly lady had poured for her. "Thank you very much for the meal and directions. You're very kind."

"You watch out fer them army fellers. Some of 'em ain't got much good in 'em."

"I will," Dixie assured her. She left the cabin and walked as fast as she could, following the directions the woman had given her.

After twenty minutes a wagon came rumbling along with a man and a woman on the seat. "Whoa, there," the man called, and when the wagon stopped, the woman, who was wearing a tattered brown coat and a bonnet pulled over her eyes, asked, "You be goin' to town?"

"I'm going to Valley Forge."

"Git in," the woman said. "It's a long walk. We're headed to the store down the road. The camp ain't far from it."

Dixie willingly climbed into the wagon and spent the next forty minutes answering questions. When they got to the small village, she got down quickly and asked, "Do you know which way it is to the camp?"

"Down that road right there, but you got to watch out. It ain't safe for a young'un to be roamin' around with a war on and all."

"I'll be careful," Dixie promised. "Thank you very much for the ride."

She turned and started down the road, hoping that another wagon would come along. After a while, an old man with a long, gray beard appeared, riding a skinny mule. He pulled up on the reins. "Whoa there, Josephine!" He looked down at Dixie and studied her for a moment. His mouth was almost hidden behind his beard, but he had a kind look in his blue eyes. "You goin' to the soldiers' camp?"

"Yes, sir, I am."

"Pretty long walk for a young'un like you. If you're keen to ride on top of old Josephine here, I'd be mighty proud to accommodate you."

Dixie could scarcely believe her good fortune, but she looked skeptically at the tall mule. The cold was beginning to turn her feet numb, and she knew in this weather she'd be crazy to pass up an offer like this. "That's very thoughtful of you. I don't know if I can get on, though. She's so tall."

The old man moved quickly. He leaned over, picked Dixie up before she could speak, and she suddenly found herself sitting on the mule, her legs dangling down the side of the lanky animal.

"Just hang on. My name's Jed—Jed Trumpet. You ain't likely to fall off Josephine. She ain't been in a hurry for fifteen years now."

Dixie found it simple to hang on. She kept one hand on the old man's waist and the other balancing on the rump of the mule. Josephine was, indeed, a slow mover, but it was wonderful to not have to walk through the cold, mushy snow. To Dixie's relief, the old man did not seem too interested in finding out why she was out in the middle of nowhere by herself.

Finally she asked him, "Do you live near the camp?"

"Yes, missy, I do. Me and my old woman, we've been in Valley Forge for over fifty years now." He reached up, pulled his hat up, and scratched his thick gray hair. "A little bit different now with all them soldiers there. Till they come, there weren't nobody but us and the critters."

"Do you think General Washington and his soldiers will win the war?"

"Don't know about that. Don't rightly know what all the fightin's about. My old woman, she studies it pretty careful. Says we're fightin' with the Britishers so we don't have to do what they tell us." He laughed aloud, and his shoulders shook. "I wasn't doin' what they told me no how. So, don't reckon it matters much to me. You got friends in the army there?"

"Yes, my brother's there. We're looking for my father."

"Lost your pap, eh? Well, hope you find him."

By the time Jed and Josephine had arrived at the collection of rude shacks and cabins, Dixie had learned a lot about her host. He was a talkative old man when he got started. When she slipped to the ground, she looked up and thanked him.

"You take care of yourself now," Jed told her.

"I will. Thank you, Mr. Trumpet." She turned and walked down the road toward the row of cabins. Almost immediately she noticed a large man wearing an officer's uniform mounted on a white horse riding toward her. He stopped and looked down at her. He had a round face, and Dixie saw that something was wrong with one of his hands. "Please, sir, can you help me? I'm looking for someone."

"Anyone in particular? I'm Colonel Henry Knox. You're not lookin' for me, are you?" he grinned happily at her.

Right away, Dixie liked him. His smile was contagious, and she noticed it lit up his entire face. "My brother and a friend of ours came to camp looking for my father some time ago. My brother's name is Danny Fortune."

"Well now, Danny is your brother! I must say it's a pleasure to meet you. What's your name?"

"Dixie Fortune."

"Well, Miss Fortune, we feel mighty lucky to have had your brother and Miss Johnson at our camp these past few weeks. They're puttin' up with the cook in one of the little huts. Come along, and I'll take you to them."

"Oh, that'll be kind of you, Colonel Knox."

Knox guided his horse slowly through the camp, and as they moved closer to the line of huts, he said, "You've got a good brother, and your friend, Miss Johnson, is a fine young lady. They've done a great work here."

"Really?" Dixie asked in surprise. *What on earth could Courtney have done that was so spectacular?*

"They've been a big help to the wounded men in the hospital," Knox explained. He proceeded to tell her how Danny and Courtney had bought supplies and had assisted the doctor the past few days.

"I'm so glad, sir," she responded quietly. Dixie had no problem imagining Danny doing something like that, but not Courtney Johnson. From what Dixie had seen of Courtney in school, she knew Courtney was a selfish and snobby girl who only cared for her own well being.

As they approached the hut, Knox stopped and said, "It's right there. The one on the end. We're glad to have you visit our camp, Miss Fortune. I trust I'll see you again."

"Thank you, Colonel Knox."

As the colonel rode away, Dixie moved toward the hut. She knocked on the door, and at once it opened. Danny stood there, and as he saw her, his face went blank with shock. "Dixie—!" he gasped.

"Hi, Danny." Dixie threw herself into his arms and hugged him hard, then stepped back to look at him. "I'll bet you didn't expect to see me here."

"I sure didn't. . . . Courtney, look who's here!"

Courtney had been cooking something over the wood fire. She straightened up and quickly walked over. "Dixie," she said with surprise. "What are you doing here?"

They pulled her in and shut the door. While Courtney made some tea for the three of them, Dixie explained everything that had happened to her up till now.

Danny listened carefully, and when Dixie showed

him the letter, he exclaimed, "Well, no wonder we haven't been able to find Dad!"

"Now we'll have to start all over," Courtney complained.

Dixie looked at Courtney carefully. Her hair was combed as best it could be, but it was still not the old Courtney. She was wearing a dirty dress, and her hands were chapped with the cold, her fingernails broken. *She looks so different. I'm surprised she let Danny stay this long*, Dixie thought. Aloud she said, "Well, it shouldn't be too hard now that we've got the right name."

"Let's hope so." Danny was beginning to perk up with the new information, forgetting how worn down he was from the days and days of little food and late nights at the hospital. "Now let's go find the quartermaster. He's got at least some of the army rolls that didn't get left behind."

They went to the headquarters at once, where they found Lieutenant Masters, the quartermaster for the Continental Army, working over his papers. He looked up and blinked as they came in. "Well, there are three of you now?"

"Yes, Lieutenant, this is my sister, Dixie Fortune. We're wondering if you have a James Dare in your rolls. We think maybe our father changed his last name for some reason. Dare was his mother's maiden name."

The three stood there as Lieutenant Masters ran through several roster books. They were all disappointed when he shook his head. "I don't find his name here."

"Isn't there anywhere else you could look, Lieutenant?" Courtney pleaded.

"Well," he said, stroking his chin, "let me see. . . . Wait a minute. There is one more place." He rummaged through his desk, found a sheaf of papers, and ran his finger down the list. "Well," he exclaimed, "there *is* a James Dare!"

Danny and Dixie both cried out in excitement.

"Well, it may not be very good news," he warned them.

"What's wrong, Lieutenant?" Dixie asked with a frightened tone in her voice.

"James Dare was enlisted in the Third Virginia Regiment, but he was captured on our retreat out of New York."

"Captured!" Danny exclaimed. "You mean he's a prisoner of the British?"

"Yes. I expect he's in one of the hulks in New York Harbor."

"A hulk? What's a hulk?" Courtney asked.

"That's just an old warship that's too old to fight, so the British make them into prisons. Pretty bad places. Men left down in the hulls—no light, no air, rats, and lots of sickness there. The wounded don't last long." He saw the expression on the faces of the young people and shrugged his shoulders. "Maybe it won't be so bad with your father."

"We've got to get to New York right away!" Danny exclaimed.

"Well, that might be a problem. Would be for a soldier, but civilians—well, I guess you could make it."

"Can you tell us how to get there?"

"Go back to that little village. There'll be a post coming through that carries the mail. If you have money, you can pay your fare with it."

Danny's face suddenly went blank. "Well, thank you. It was nice of you, Lieutenant Masters."

A bit dejected, Danny turned and walked out, and as soon as Dixie and Courtney caught up with him, he admitted, "We spent all our money on food and supplies for the wounded men! We'll have to walk to New York."

"No, we won't." Dixie reached into her pocket and brought out the bag of gold coins that their uncles had given her for the trip.

Danny stared at his sister, then let out a loud whoop. Throwing his arm around her, he picked her up and swung her around in a circle. "Sis, you're amazing!"

"Put me down, you nut! You're going to squeeze me to death!"

When Danny set her down, she felt a touch on her arm and turned to see that Courtney had a smile on her face. "It was very brave of you to come."

"Oh, I don't know about that," Dixie mumbled. She wondered to herself what was going on with Courtney. All Dixie knew about her was that she was a spoiled brat who always got her own way. Now she seemed to be at least a little nice.

"You know, I think we ought to say good-bye to General Washington before we leave," Danny said.

"I think we found out where my father is, General Washington." Danny was glad to finally have a lead, but at the same time he was going to miss the general. Talking to a great historical figure was an amazing experience.

"Well, I'm glad to hear that. Was he with our men?" the general inquired. He had come to his feet and towered over them now. He had met Dixie, and when they told him that James Dare was in a prison ship, he shook his head. "I'm grieved to hear that, but at least he's alive."

"We're going to leave right away for New York. I wanted to thank you for all your help and kindness, General."

"I wish I could have done more," George Washington said. He shook hands with all three of them as he said, "May God go with you on your journeys. I trust you'll find your father, but this is not going to be a short war." His face was troubled. "I wish there were some way I could help. Perhaps an exchange could be worked out."

"What kind of an exchange?" Courtney inquired.

"Oh, it's very simple. We capture the British, and

they capture us, and from time to time we take the men that we've captured of theirs and give them back, and they give us an equal number of our men."

"Do you think that might be possible?" Dixie asked hopefully.

"It's very difficult and takes a long time. Besides, they have so many more of our men than we have of theirs. I'm afraid I can't offer you much hope."

"Well, I know God will work things out," Danny said stoutly. He shook the general's hand, then the three of them left the headquarters.

"Well, one more stop," Courtney said.

"Where's that?" Danny asked.

"I want to go say good-bye to Nathaniel. Will you get my things while I do that?"

"Sure. We'll be ready when you are."

Courtney found Dr. Simmons pleased to see her, as always. "How's our patient today, doctor?"

"I'm fine."

Courtney wheeled around, and surprise washed over her face as she saw Nathaniel Bates standing, holding on to a cane that had been carved from a tree limb. He was smiling, and there was a healthy glow in his cheeks.

"Nathaniel, you're up!" Courtney breathed. She went to him quickly and took the hand he held out.

"Well, I'm up, all right. The room's swimming a little bit, but I'm up."

"He's doing fine, Miss Johnson," Dr. Simmons assured her. He seemed to be very pleased at his patient's quick recovery. "You'd make a fine nurse."

"You sure would," Nathaniel agreed. He was thin, but there was a brightness in his eyes as he said, "I'm gonna make it, Miss Courtney."

"I'm so glad, Nathaniel, but—" She hesitated, then said, "I've come to say good-bye. My friends and I are leaving."

Nathaniel's face grew sober. "Well, I'm sorry to hear that." Then he suddenly brightened. "But you sure did come at the right time for me—and for a lot more of these fellas."

"The men will never forget you, Miss Johnson," Dr. Simmons said as he came over to shake her hand. He bowed and kissed her hand, which brought a flush to her face. "You are a fine young lady, and I know that the Lord brought you to this place."

Courtney flushed. "I believe you're right, doctor. It's been an unforgettable experience for me."

She shook hands with the doctor, gave Nathaniel a hug, and after a final glance, turned and left the hospital.

When Courtney reached the hut, Dixie and Danny

had already loaded their meager possessions on the wagon.

"Come on, Courtney. You can sit between Dixie and me."

Courtney climbed into the wagon, and Dixie seated herself next to her.

"Get up there, horse!" Danny commanded, and the wagon moved out.

They were silent as they left the camp at Valley Forge, all of them looking at the men who were hungry and poorly clothed.

"I don't want to think about them like this," Courtney said softly.

"Well, according to the history books, this winter made the Continental Army a fighting force," Danny said. "They got a German named VanStruben who came and taught the men how to drill. General Greene became the quartermaster, and he managed to get good supplies. If you could see this place in the spring, Courtney, you'd see a bunch of healthy, well-fed, well-clothed soldiers moving out, and they whipped the British."

"What's happened to you, Courtney?" Dixie asked abruptly. "You're so—well, so different."

Courtney didn't answer for a moment as she thought about how to reply. "I think the difference is I let Jesus into my heart."

"You did!" Dixie exclaimed. "How did it happen?"

The twins listened as Courtney explained how her heart had been touched by the chaplain's prayer, then how she seemed to feel God speaking to her. Finally she said, "I did what the chaplain said. I asked Jesus to come into my heart, and I think He has. I feel so different."

Danny suddenly put his arm around her and gave her a squeeze. "I'm so glad to hear it."

"It's going to be different when you go back to school, you know," Dixie warned her. "People might make fun of you."

"They'll just have to live with it," Courtney said firmly, a smile stuck on her face.

11

Danny sold the wagon and horse at the village, and the three got a place on the post stage for New York. The journey was hard and difficult. Halfway there they encountered a brief snowstorm that forced them to stay two days at a rather grimy inn. They were fortunate, however, in that there were few other travelers, and the girls managed to get a room with a double bed.

As they approached New York on the fifth day, Danny turned to look at Dixie, who was sitting on his right, staring out the window. "It would have been a lot easier if Dad had been at Valley Forge."

Taking her eyes off the countryside, which was mostly barren and gray, Dixie shrugged. "We've come this far, and at least we found out where Dad is. No matter what it takes to get Dad back, God's going to be with us every step of the way."

Courtney, who was seated across from Danny, studied the pair. She was thinking about all she had been through over the last several days, and how much she had learned. For starters, she was finally beginning to understand what it meant to be a true friend. Not one that used others for the sole purpose of getting something from them, but a friend that was there for you, someone you could trust. Courtney was thankful that she was even beginning to be closer with Dixie. She sat there quietly, thinking of the changes that had come into her life—and those that were yet to come.

Danny and Dixie had talked about Courtney in the few spare moments they had alone together. They were both very surprised at how much she had changed. Now, noticing her silence, Danny finally said, "What are you thinking about, Courtney? You haven't said a word for the last hour."

Shifting uncomfortably in the seat, Courtney reached up and tucked a curl into her bonnet. "Well, of course I'm concerned about getting your father out of prison, but when we finally go back home I'm wondering how my parents are going to take it—my becoming a Christian."

"Don't they ever talk to you about God? Don't you go to church?" Dixie inquired.

"No. They never say anything about prayer or God, and we only go to church maybe once or twice a year. Usually at Christmas or Easter."

Dixie leaned forward and patted Courtney's hand. "It'll be fine, Courtney. You'll see."

For a while Danny talked about the fun things they could do when they got back home. Then he heard the driver call out, "New York stop ahead!"

Forty minutes later they stepped down from the

coach. Danny was gathering their meager baggage together and said to the girls, "I guess the first thing we do is get a place to stay, just in case we can't get to Dad today."

At a nearby inn, Dixie and Courtney were able to get a room with a bed to themselves, and Danny got a room of his own. As soon as they were settled, Danny said, "I think we'd better go to the British authorities here."

"Are you going to tell them the truth?"

"Well, not about coming back in time, but I can tell them James Dare is our father. Hopefully, that will be all they need to hear for us to get in to see him."

The British headquarters was located in an old brownstone mansion close to the dock. Only Danny went in, and the lieutenant who finally received him was a tall, snooty-looking man. When Danny told him what he wanted, he sneered. "Your father's a rebel, is he?" He lectured him for some time on the evils of rebelling against one's king and one's country, but he finally ran his eye down a list of prisoners. "Well, he's there, all right. You'll find him in one of the hulks. The name of it's the *Empire*."

"Can we go on board and see him?"

"One of you can," the lieutenant said. He made out a pass, handed it to Danny, and said, "No women allowed on board, or girls, and you can only see him for a few minutes. This pass is only good for one trip."

"Thank you, sir." Danny forced himself to smile. He turned, left the building, and walked outside where he found Dixie and Courtney waiting anxiously. "Well, he's on the ship *Empire*—one of the hulks in the harbor." He held up the slip of paper. "I've got a pass, but it's only good for one person and only for one time."

"That's no good!" Dixie exclaimed with disappointment on her face. "We've all got to be together when we go back."

"That's right," Danny said. "We'll have to think of something."

They walked along the street slowly, trying to come up with a plan. Suddenly, Courtney's eyes brightened. "I think I know something that might work!"

"If you have any ideas at all, it's better than what's on my mind, which is nothing. What are you thinking?" asked Dixie.

"Why don't we make a copy of this, only we change it a little bit?"

"You mean forge another pass?" Danny questioned.

"Yes. Look, he wrote it right at the top of this paper. We could cut the paper in two," Courtney explained eagerly, "and write another pass down on the bottom."

"They might recognize the officer's handwriting," Danny protested.

"We'll have to practice and be very careful, then make the pass exactly like this one. Maybe we can trace it all. Look, it says, *Admit one visitor to the prison ship* Empire. *Visitor is to see the prisoner James Dare,* and then his signature."

"Maybe you're right, Courtney!" Dixie said. "All we have to do on the second one is change it so it says to admit three visitors, and then we can all go aboard."

"You can't do that," Danny said. "First of all, forging a pass isn't exactly legal, you know. And second, they don't let women or girls on board the prison ships."

Stunned into silence, the two girls looked at each other for a moment, then Courtney quietly said, "I think this might be our only chance, Danny. There's no other way for all of us to get on the ship without a pass that will allow three visitors. As for the *no girls allowed* policy . . . we'll think of something. Danny, I think you ought to go see your father and get him ready. Then when we all go on board, we can go back home together."

"Okay," Danny said reluctantly. "Let's go work on this pass. We have to do it perfectly, though. If they catch us, they'll probably throw us all in jail," he warned.

"They won't catch us," Dixie said confidently. "Come on, Courtney, we'll work on the pass while Danny thinks of some way to explain all this to Dad."

The three went back to the inn, where they spent an hour forging a new pass. "Sure would be nice if we could all go in at once," Danny said.

Suddenly, Dixie looked up, inspiration showing on her face. "If they won't let girls in, then we'll just have to become boys."

Danny and Courtney stared at her in surprise. "What do you mean by that?" Danny said.

Courtney suddenly laughed with realization. "I know what she means. We'll have to dress up like boys."

"You mean cut your hair off?"

"If we have to," Courtney said nervously, "but maybe we can get some kind of a cap we can pin our hair up in and fasten the hat over it."

Danny shook his head. "It'd be tricky, but at least it's an idea."

"Come on, Courtney. Let's go buy some boys' clothing. We've got just about enough money left to do that and to maybe bribe a guard or two," Dixie said brightly.

The two girls left for their shopping trip, and Danny stayed at the inn, thinking about his father and what had to be done.

He was sitting in his own room when he heard a knock. Opening the door, he peered and burst out laughing. "Well, you're the two prettiest boys I ever saw!"

Dixie and Courtney had donned boys' baggy clothing and done their best to conceal their hair under caps. "You better smear some dirt on your face." He supervised that operation, then finally looked at them and said, "With those pants you're wearing, no one will suspect a thing. You look good enough, but you better remember not to say a word. You don't sound like boys."

"We can do it, Danny," Dixie assured him. "Let's get going."

Danny took a deep breath. "All right. I guess the sooner, the better. You got the pass ready?"

"Yes. It's right here." Courtney handed the forged pass over to Danny.

He studied it carefully and took a deep breath. "Well, it looks as good as the other one to me. I hope they don't notice it's just on half a sheet of paper." He looked at them and licked his lips nervously. "This is the hardest thing we've ever tried to do, I think."

The harbor was full of ships, and it took them an hour to find the *Empire*. It was almost the last ship in the line, and they could smell it even before they got there.

"Boy, everything smells awful!"

"Well, they probably don't have any sanitation at all," Dixie said in a whisper. "Come on. Let's get it over with."

As they moved down the harbor, Danny said, "It looks like we'll have to get a boat to carry us out. I've got just a little money left. I hope it's enough."

"Well, we won't need any more after this." Dixie

peered nervously out at the old ship, which was rotten with age and looked almost ready to sink.

"There's a small boat with a man sitting beside it over there," Courtney said. "Maybe he could take us."

"Let's ask. Come on," Danny commanded.

They walked up to the man, and Danny said, "Hello. We need to hire a boat to take us out to that ship—the *Empire*."

"Take hard cash. No Continental," the man replied. He was a middle-aged man, husky and bull-shouldered, with a pair of fair blue eyes.

They settled on the price, and the man insisted on payment beforehand. "I've got the coin." Danny took it out of his pocket.

"Get in," he ordered. "I'll row you out."

The three of them got into the boat, and the boatman shoved them off. Leaping behind the oars, he began to pull with slow, steady strokes. "You got a relative out on the hulk?" he asked.

"Yes, our father."

"Ahh, too bad." He started to say something else but saw the faces of the young people and kept it to himself. When he pulled up beside the old ship, he greeted them by saying, "Ahoy, *Empire*! Visitors for a prisoner!"

A ladder was built onto the side of the ship, and the boatman held the boat steady. "Watch your step, boys!"

Danny went first and had to stop himself from

turning to help the girls. *That wouldn't look right*, he thought to himself.

A man was waiting at the top, dressed in a British uniform. "You got a pass?" he asked gruffly.

"Yes, sir." Danny handed him the pass, then they all held their breath as the man read it.

The officer shook his head. "I never heard of three visitors to a prisoner. How come that?"

"Well, we're family. We'd like to see our father together," Danny explained.

The eyes of the officer softened as Danny's words came out, and he nodded in response.

"Could we see our father alone? It would be worth some money to us." He held out a single gold coin, and the officer's eyes glittered.

Immediately the officer plucked it out of Danny's fingers and stuffed it in his waistcoat. "Well," he cleared his throat again and nodded, "I see no harm in that. Come along." He led them along the deck, then down a ladder to a lower deck. It was dark and gloomy, and the smell was horrible. He opened a door and said, "Here, this is my own quarters. You stay here, and I'll get the prisoner."

They stepped inside and looked around at the cabin, which was illuminated by a single candle.

"I'd hate to live in this place," Courtney said. "It's awful."

They all stood nervously waiting for what seemed like a long time, and then they heard footsteps. The door opened, and the officer called out, "You got twenty minutes. Be quick now!"

Danny and Dixie stared at the man who stepped inside. He was dirty and haggard and was dressed in rags, and he smelled awful. His beard had grown out and covered the lower part of his face, and his hair was long—but it definitely was their father.

"Who is it?" James said, blinking his eyes against the feeble light of the candle. "Who is in here?"

"Dad, it's me, Dixie!" She threw herself forward and put her arms around the thin body of her father, squeezing him as tears came to her eyes.

"Dixie? It can't be you!" He held his daughter close, then his eyes became more accustomed to the light, and he saw the young man standing before him. "Danny! It's you!"

"It's really us, Dad. We've come to take you back."

James Fortune stood there holding his two children. His arms around them both, he whispered, "Thank God. I've prayed for this every day, but it's been a long wait."

Dixie pulled back and said, "Dad, this is Courtney Johnson, one of our friends."

"I'm glad to meet you, Courtney. You're a brave girl to come back and help Dixie and Danny find me."

"Dad, we don't have time to talk." Danny stepped back but held his father by the arm.

"Did you bring the Recall Unit?" Mr. Fortune's eyes were bright with hope, and he didn't seem able to get enough of the sight of his two children.

"I've got it right here." Danny pulled the Recall

Unit from under his shirt by the leather cord. "We've never used it with four people, but it should work."

"Come here, Courtney," Dixie said. "Let's all stand arm in arm."

Courtney came over at once and took Dixie's arm. The four got as close together as possible, and James smiled with pride at his children. "I'm mighty proud of you. I know this was hard. Now let's go home."

Danny pushed the button on the Recall Unit, and instantly a faint humming seemed to fill the small room. A green glow enveloped the four, and Danny felt himself dissolving. "Here we go!" he cried. "Back to the good old United States of America!"

Courtney held tightly to Dixie's arm. She was a little afraid, but a gladness at what had happened to her on this journey overpowered her fear.

They all felt the vibration increase, and the cabin seemed to disappear.

12

Danny and Dixie had already made two arrivals coming back from their previous time travels—but this time it was completely different. Always before there had been the soft, light green glow and the faint humming of the Chrono-Shuttle.

Now as Danny felt himself coming out of one world into another, he heard the sound of things breaking, of wreckage of some kind, and he screamed, "Something's gone wrong!"

"I don't like this at all!" Dixie yelled back. "It feels like we're being shaken to pieces!"

Courtney, who had never experienced a return to the present, clung to Danny and shut her eyes. The sound of breaking glass filled her ears, and she held her breath while she waited for whatever was happening around her to end.

James Fortune, weak as he was from his long imprisonment, held on to Danny and Dixie with a fierce grip. As the shaking and sound of breakage grew stronger, he opened his eyes. At first he could not make out what he was looking at, but then he saw the familiar form of the laboratory beginning to take shape. He could also see that the Chrono-Shuttle was spitting sparks out of its control panel. Looking up, he saw that the entire laboratory was filled with what looked like miniature bolts of lightning that flickered over the instruments. It looked like something out of a mad-scientist movie, and he held his children closer. "Hang on! I think we've almost made it!"

A sudden, violent jolt, and the four were thrown around in the shuttle. It collapsed, and the doors popped off so that Danny and Courtney rolled out one side, James and Dixie out the other. They all scrambled to their feet and stood with their backs against the laboratory walls, looking around in a daze. The miniature lightning bolts were still flickering over parts of the equipment, and the floor was covered with what used to be the Chrono-Shuttle.

As James glanced around to his left, he saw Zacharias Fortune shoving one of the shuttle's doors off of himself, kicking at it wildly and springing to his feet. His eyes were wide with horror, and he screamed, "What's gone wrong?"

Across the room Mordecai Fortune, who had taken refuge behind a concrete pillar, poked his head around. He was too stunned by what had happened to speak.

Zacharias began pulling at his hair. It looked as though he was trying to lift himself off the floor. "Look what you've done to my machine!" he cried. "My beautiful machine!" He ran over and picked up a part of the Chrono-Shuttle and looked hopelessly around at the mess in despair. "It's gone . . . all gone."

Dixie looked up at her father, then turned to her uncles. "But we're all back safe and alive. We finally found Dad! That's something, isn't it?"

"It certainly is something," James said, trying to sound positive.

Mordecai turned to stare at him and said, "James! You actually made it!"

"Yep. My kids came through for me—and so did you and Uncle Zacharias."

"Come on, Dad," Dixie said, tugging on his sleeve. "We'll get you cleaned up while Uncle Mordecai has Toombs fix you something to eat."

Mordecai was so stunned by the destruction of the Chrono-Shuttle and the entire lab, he could only nod.

"Would it be all right if we use your bathroom, Uncle Zacharias? Dad needs to shave and shower."

Zacharias Fortune cast his eyes around at the wreckage, and his shoulders slumped. The life seemed to have gone out of him, and he moaned, "All that work—now it's all gone!"

"He's not going to do anything but cry over his machine, Dad," Danny said. "Come on. I know where a bathroom is, and I think we can dig up an electric razor somewhere in there."

Dixie, who went over to comfort Zacharias, asked softly, "You can build it back, can't you?"

"No. Never! It took nearly a lifetime to build it!" He ran his hands through his hair. "What on earth happened? Was it something in the Recall Unit? Too many coming back, perhaps?" Zacharias questioned almost frantically.

"We may never know," Mordecai answered in a whisper.

When James and Danny returned, both wearing the clothes they had on before their trips, James added his own conclusions about the damaged Chrono-Shuttle.

"I think the whole thing was a mistake to begin with. It isn't good to be fooling around with time the way we've been doing."

"But what's wrong with it?" Zacharias demanded.

"What's past is past!" James said firmly. "I would never go back again. Not even if the machine weren't broken. You're a wonderful inventor, Zacharias, but you need to turn your talents to something that would be of more use to the world for the future."

"I think Dad's right, Uncle Zacharias," Danny said quickly. "Just think of the damage that could be done. For instance, if Dad had died back there, Dixie and I would never have been born because he wouldn't be here to be our father."

Zacharias would have once argued violently, but the destruction of the machine and his laboratory sobered him. He moaned and put his head in his hands. "What am I going to do now?"

"I have some ideas," James said. "Some things that

the world really needs. I'd like to work on these ideas with you and Uncle Mordecai. We could do great things together."

"Do you really think so?" Zacharias lifted his head and seemed to cheer up. "What are some of your ideas?"

"I can't tell you now. I've got to get home to see my wife," James said. "I've been away for a very long time."

"Only about a week in our time, Dad." Danny looked at his watch and then grinned at Courtney. "It seemed like a long time that we were in Valley Forge, but according to our time, we've only been gone for three hours."

"Come on, Courtney," Dixie said. "Let's change back into our regular clothes. I'm sick of this wool dress, and I'm already starting to sweat."

After changing, they walked to the front door and told the uncles good-bye, James Fortune assuring them both that he would call them soon so they could begin working on some new ideas.

Courtney's car was still parked out in the driveway, and Mr. Fortune took the driver's seat. On their way home, Dixie and Danny told their father what wonderful things Courtney had done for the men in the hospital—especially Nathaniel Bates.

James Fortune looked in the rearview mirror, and

as he caught Danny's eye, he winked. Although he had never met Courtney before, he remembered the enormous crush Danny had always had on the girl.

They pulled up in front of the apartment building the Fortunes lived in, and as they all got out of the car, Courtney walked over and hugged Dixie. Then she suddenly leaned forward and kissed Danny on the cheek. "I love both of you," she beamed. "I will never forget this adventure. And in the future, I don't think I'll *ever* doubt anything you tell me, Danny, no matter how crazy it sounds!" Then she got into her car and roared off.

"Well, you certainly made an impression on her," Dad said as they walked toward their building.

"I guess so," Danny mumbled. His cheek was still tingling from the kiss.

"Your mother is going to be a little surprised," James said as they stood in front of the door to the apartment.

That was putting it mildly!

Ellen Fortune had come home and was in the kitchen making a cake. She heard the door open and called out, "Dixie, you are in big trouble, young lady. I don't know where you've been this afternoon, but you'd better have a good excuse! You're still sick, you know."

Dixie winked at her father. "Actually, I've got a surprise for you, Mom!" she called out.

"Yeah, kind of an early birthday present," Danny added. "Come and get it!"

Ellen Fortune appeared in the doorway with a sauce pan in one hand and a wooden spoon in the other. As soon as she saw her husband, she froze. She let out a scream, then dropped the sauce pan, sending chocolate cake batter all over the carpet. "James!" she cried and ran toward him.

James Fortune caught his wife in his arms and lifted her off her feet.

"You're home! You're home!" Ellen cried.

"Some birthday present, huh, Mom?" Danny grinned.

The twins stood there watching them, then another voice said, "Daddy! You're home!"

James looked around to see Jimmy, and his heart leaped. "Come here, son. I've missed you so much!" He took in the dark blue eyes and shiny blond hair, and as he held his youngest in his arms, he turned and said, "I think we ought to give thanks to God that we're back safe."

"That's a good idea," Danny said. He waited until his father had prayed, then said, "Mom, why don't we all go out and celebrate!"

"I want to go to McDonald's and get a cheeseburger with extra large fries," Jimmy announced.

"That's not celebrating! We do that all the time!" Dixie said in disgust.

"We'll go there first and get that for Jimmy, then we'll go someplace else for the rest of us," James said.

"James, where have you been all this time?" Ellen finally asked once the initial shock began to wear off.

Seeing the questioning look in her eyes, James knew he had a lot of explaining to do. He looked at Danny and Dixie, sending both of them a secretive wink. "It's a long story, Ellen. Too long to tell before supper. I'll talk about it when we get there. But I will say this—I missed you more than you could ever imagine!"

13

Tom Benton was standing with a group of his friends, most of whom he played football with. He looked up and saw Courtney Johnson coming down the hall. "Watch this," he told them smugly.

Benton swaggered over toward Courtney and drawled, "Hi, Courtney."

"Hello, Tom."

Courtney would have kept walking, but Tom took her arm and said, "I gotta talk to you."

"We'll be late for class."

"Ahh, who cares? Mrs. Simpkins won't do anything to us."

"I'd really rather be on time, if you don't mind."

"Wait a minute! Just listen to what I have to say." He pulled her around and looked down at her. "This is your lucky day. I've been thinking that maybe you and I ought to go out to eat tonight."

Benton obviously expected Courtney to fall over herself accepting his offer. Instead, she looked at him and said coolly, "Thanks, Tom, but I'm just not interested." She pulled away from his grasp and walked down the hall.

Jason Bledsoe, who had been standing close enough to hear Courtney's response, cackled, "Nice work, Romeo."

"This ain't over yet!" Benton blustered. "I'll have her eatin' out of my hand before you know it. Come on, let's go to class."

Inside Mrs. Simpkins' class the students were getting settled. Courtney smiled at Danny, who was already there, and he smiled back at her. There was no chance to talk, though, because the bell had rung. As the latecomers settled into their chairs, Mrs. Simpkins scolded them. "All right, quiet down! Now let me check the roll."

The class was still talking about the Revolutionary War. Danny had to remind himself that it had only been one day since he had last sat here in this room. They had been at Valley Forge for such a long time that it felt like weeks later in the present. As Mrs. Simpkins began the class, Danny remembered the freezing cold of the cook's hut that he and Courtney had stayed in, how their fingers and lips had turned blue—so numb they could hardly move their fingers or speak. He looked over at Courtney and saw that she was smiling at him, her head turned sideways.

After the bell rang, Courtney got up and gathered her books. Tom Benton was at her side immediately, saying loudly, "Hey, Courtney! You and me, how does Chinese food sound for tonight?"

Courtney looked at the big football player and smiled sweetly. "I already told you no, Tom. I'm sorry."

She turned then and took Danny's arm, who had come down the aisle toward her. "Danny and I have other plans."

Benton's friends had waited around to see what would happen, and now Tom's face flamed as he glared at Danny. "You'd turn me down for a wimp like this?"

Courtney tightened her grip on Danny's arm and said, "It may take a lot of strength to play football, Tom, but Danny has something you'll never have— guts."

Tom was still mumbling as Courtney drew Danny out of the classroom.

"That was sweet of you, Courtney." Dixie had joined them and was still laughing over the shocked expression on Tom's face.

"Did you mean it? Do we really have other plans?" Danny asked.

"Yes. You and Dixie are coming over to my house. I want you to meet my parents."

Danny looked into Courtney's beautiful blue eyes. "That sounds great. A lot better than freezing at Valley Forge."

The mention of Valley Forge made them all quiet for a minute until Courtney said, "I can't ever be sorry we went there. We found your father . . . and I found Jesus!"

The three of them looked at one another with satisfaction, turned, and walked down the hall.

Teen Series From
Bethany House Publishers

***

Early Teen Fiction (11–14)

HIGH HURDLES by Lauraine Snelling
Show jumper DJ Randall strives to defy the odds and achieve her dream of winning Olympic Gold.

SUMMERHILL SECRETS by Beverly Lewis
Fun-loving Merry Hanson encounters mystery and excitement in Pennsylvania's Amish country.

THE TIME NAVIGATORS by Gilbert Morris
Travel back in time with Danny and Dixie as they explore unforgettable moments in history.

Young Adult Fiction (12 and up)

CEDAR RIVER DAYDREAMS by Judy Baer
Experience the challenges and excitement of high school life with Lexi Leighton and her friends—over one million books sold!

GOLDEN FILLY SERIES by Lauraine Snelling
Readers are in for an exhilarating ride as Tricia Evanston races to become the first female jockey to win the sought-after Triple Crown.

JENNIE McGRADY MYSTERIES by Patricia Rushford
A contemporary Nancy Drew, Jennie McGrady's sleuthing talents promise to keep readers on the edge of their seats.

LIVE! FROM BRENTWOOD HIGH by Judy Baer
When eight teenagers invade the newsroom, the result is an action-packed teen-run news show exploring the love, laughter, and tears of high school life.

THE SPECTRUM CHRONICLES by Thomas Locke
Adventure and romance await readers in this fantasy series set in another place and time.

SPRINGSONG BOOKS by various authors
Compelling love stories and contemporary themes promise to capture the hearts of readers.

WHITE DOVE ROMANCES by Yvonne Lehman
Romance, suspense, and fast-paced action for teens committed to finding pure love.

9608